REUNION

OF THE

GOOD

WEATHER

SUICIDE

CULT

REUNION OF THE GOOD WEATHER SUICIDE CULT

KYLE MCCORD

atmosphere press

A GUIDE TO CHARACTER NAMES

Given Name	Name in the Good Weather Community
Tom Duncan	Ohio
Lisa Duncan	Allegheny (Alle)
Leonard Fairbanks	Rain
Katie Hunt	Thames
Gerald Benson	Atlantic
Elise Hernandez	Rio Grande (Rio)

PART 1

CHAPTER 1

From the 2020 Netflix Documentary Series *The Good Weather* "Episode 9: Burnt Bones and Bean Hooks"

(The episode opens with a police officer seated before a black drape cloth background. He wears a navy suit and raps a digit against his chair impatiently. A caption identifies him as "Detective Dodson, Edenburg P.D.")

Detective Dodson: "The first thing you need to understand is that I do this for a living: I size people up, observe their body language, notice their tics. Does the subject press a finger to their lips when their deceased spouse is mentioned? Or do they stiffen their limbs? When they tell their side of the story what subtle details shift over time? Do they narrate what happened like they've rehearsed it?

"So, what do I think about Tom Duncan? The man's a liar. He knows more than he's saying, and he's spinning a version of events that makes him sound like a lamb to the slaughter. But don't believe a word of that bullshit. While the department may not be able to connect Tom Duncan with the doping of the water supply or the perpetration of the mass suicide itself, it is my firm belief that he was a part of the plot, not a victim of it. Period."

(A montage plays of a verdant cornfield. Above it, wind turbines slice at the air like a hoe severing the body of a garden snake. The shots of Iowa exude serenity. The camera captures the moment of dawn before the land is animate with a traffic of machinery rolling between the stalks. A singular motorist passes on the highway.)

Detective Dodson: "Consider this: very few community members were allowed to communicate with anyone not currently at the Good Weather compound. Cult leaders keep tight reins on the flow of information, and Leonard Fairbanks, aka 'Rain,' was a cult dictator extraordinaire. The compound was on 24/7 lockdown.

"But you know who had easy access to email in his cushy office in the Atoll? Tom Duncan. And we have evidence that for months before the suicide, someone, using Tom's computer, emailed back and forth with Lindsey Stenson, who supplied all the drugs to lace the community water supply. If Rain, acting alone, sent those emails, why not use his own computer? Accessing Tom's only increased the odds of someone finding out. It doesn't add up."

(Fuzzy police camera footage of a middle-aged man in thick-rimmed glasses plays. Unshaven, gray hair frames his pudgy countenance; he wears a weathered wind-breaker. A fresh-faced public defender sits beside him. Dodson hunches forward in his chair, his back to the camera. The caption reads "Police interview with Tom Duncan, aka 'Ohio.'")

Dodson: "Let's cut to the chase here: what was your role in the plot to spike the Good Weather community water supply with hallucinogens?"

Lawyer: "Let me be clear. My client has, against my strong objections, agreed to answer your questions related to the mass suicide. As evidence has already made clear, Tom Duncan is a victim, not a perpetrator. We expect him to be treated as such."

Dodson: "I'm not sure the evidence is so clear cut. We have a series of missing emails between someone and Lindsey Stenson. And those emails were sent from your client's computer. Don't you find that suspicious?"

Ohio: "I didn't send them. It's as simple as that."

Dodson: "Well, I'd love to ask Stenson about that, but she killed herself as soon as the evidence implicated her."

Lawyer: "And in her suicide note, she confessed everything, including how she conspired with Leonard Fairbanks under duress. She made no mention of my client. Hell, I doubt she even knew who he was."

Dodson: "So why did she scrub all her devices and lock every account she had before she did the deed, huh? Why bother? Digital forensics is still at work to recover what we can. What are we gonna find, Tom?"

(The footage freezes for a moment then the documentary switches to a fly-by shot of the Good Weather property. A chapel spire juts toward the camera. Dorms in the style of a 1970's summer camp form even, parallel lines. Trees serving as windbreaks dot the landscape. It is orderly and devoid of any signs of life.)

Dodson: "If the missing emails sent from Tom's computer aren't damning enough, there's also his activities the day before the suicide. According to witnesses, at roughly 8:25 a.m. on August 6th, Tom Duncan arrived in the south field and ordered the work crew to purchase supplies from Menards an hour away in Waterloo.

"Once the work crew truck left the camp, we're forced to speculate about what happened. Tracks indicate multiple parties at the Atoll, where Tom worked, wheeled carts of something quite heavy out of the building. Officers followed the tracks to the south field where they discovered a metal burn barrel. Whatever was in the barrel was scorched. The entire area was carefully sanitized. We believe what the parties involved burned were financial documents from the last two decades.

"Now, why did Duncan personally send the work crews away right before this little bonfire? In my experience, innocent people don't burn documents. My guess: he was complicit in funneling money to Fairbanks' little side project."

(The documentary cuts back to the police interview. Tom covers his mouth with his hand as though his disgust might fly from his body like an exorcised demon. The dim lights in the grey room hum.)

Dodson: (leaning back in his chair) "So, what's with all the missing ledgers and spreadsheets from your HQ? Didn't want anyone on the outside seeing who was pulling the strings before you left for *Shamayin*?"

Ohio: (Muttering) *"Shamayim."*

Dodson: "What was that?"

Lawyer: "I would like to talk with my client briefly."

Ohio: "I'm not even responding to this crap. I'm just telling him that he's saying the word wrong. 'Im,' not 'in.' *Shamayim*. The two waters. Heaven."

Dodson: "Did Rain tell you to burn the financials, or was that all you? Maybe you took it upon yourself to keep the boss man happy. Makes sense. Rain was a murderous psycho; who would fault you?"

Ohio: "I told you that I had nothing to do with any of that. Rain came to my bunk and asked me to send the workers away. I didn't know why. I was scheduled for the late shift at Atoll, not morning."

Dodson: "Do you have any verification?" (Before Tom can respond) "Oh, of course not; it all went up in flames."

(The documentary switches to phone footage of several young women waving from the deck of a rustic porch. Some carry Tupperware entrees and desserts.)

Dodson: "To my mind, here's the real nail in the coffin. This is how two-faced Tom Duncan is: they're one day away from mass suicide, and what is he up to? He and other members of Good Weather are on the lawn of the chapel picnicking. Field workers, who Duncan sent away while he did his dirty business, report the congregation was celebrating. Celebrating! They were makin' cold cut sandwiches and dishin' up pasta salad. Teams played cornhole. They were singing hymns. Children brought dual heaven cookies, a treat in the Good Weather community, to some of the field workers.

"Duncan's drugged all these people; he's about to slit their throats; and he's out there having a field day with 'em. Whooping it up."

(A tan young man who a caption identifies as "Jared, field worker, 2018-2019" speaks to the camera. He sports an American flag bandana stained with sweat.)

Jared: "Seemed like they were having a holiday or something. Rain made the rounds and prayed with people. They put blankets on the lawn and ate, chatted, whatever. The kids who brought us cookies told us that they were working on some topiary project as a community.

Sounded lame, but that wasn't any weirder than most of the shit they did.

"Half my fuckin' job was not asking what they were up to. You had to put up with a looooong prayer at the start of the day, and you didn't want to pal around with any of them. But they were super friendly, and they paid good. And they didn't treat you like shit, which is more than I can say for half the farmers in Edenburg.

"Rules were strict. They didn't care if you cussed or whatever, but if you uttered word one about Rain, you were done. Like, they paid you for the day, and you were out on your ass, even if you'd been doing it a decade. One guy, they wouldn't even give him a ride back to town. I saw that idiot still walking on my drive home. I'm serious. No one wanted to pick him up because they'd fire us, too.

"Once I heard on the news about the bean hooks or whatever, once I heard what they did with them, I was like 'Oh no.'" (He pauses.) "You replay it over and over in your mind. Hearing those kids talk about sharpening bean hooks like it was the most normal thing in the world...but what could I have done even if I'd known?

"Honestly, it keeps me up at night. Everyone who worked for them, it keeps us up."

(The camera lingers long enough to see Jared grow mute. It comes in for a close-up; he looks curiously older. He turns his head and stares away from the set, his eyes appearing to pass over some object invisible to the audience. Don Burlington, the director, begins to narrate.)

Burlington: "Within thirty hours, all but one of the one hundred and thirty-seven members of the Good Weather community would be dead in one of most grisly mass-suicides in U.S. history. But to any onlooker, even those living one town over, on August 6th, the camp appeared the same as it did on any other day. The sun shone on the families who passed out sandwiches, laughing, some tossing beanbags in the air. And here and there, one person or another, sometimes a child, worked a blade to a serrated sharpness."

CHAPTER 2

More than a year after his interview with the Eden County Sheriff's Department, Tom Duncan drew the curtains over the window of his daughter's Des Moines apartment. His daughter had furnished the space sparsely, but in comparison to his shared room at the Midwest Cult Recovery Center, this was luxury living. He traced his fingers over the thick emerald damask.

A few weeks after he'd been discharged from the hospital, Anna replaced the thin muslin curtains with more concealing material. Paparazzi—if they could even be called that in so small a city—rarely mustered the balls to come directly to the window. But his daughter, Anna, left nothing to chance since the press had been bloodhounds of late. Anna told him that he needed to contain himself, that any slip would only bring more unwanted publicity. She was right, of course. He knew.

Susan, his Cult Recovery Center chaperone, had assumed a chair by the door. Tom hovered briefly by the window before navigating the minefield of play food and stuffed animals to retake his seat in the recliner at the far end of the living room.

Terra Sue, his granddaughter, looked up from her coloring book.

"Posicle?"

"It's only ten a.m., sweetie. We're coming up on lunch in an hour," replied Tom.

"I hungy," said Terra. She rose from her crouch, took Tom's hand, and pulled toward the kitchen. At first, Tom playfully resisted, but Terra tugged then implored him with her eyes. They were the same malachite gems as Anna. Same as Alle, his wife.

Tom allowed himself to be led past the table with neatly sorted baskets of mail, into the cheap laminate kitchen. He silently lamented his inability to contribute, aside from childcare, but his notoriety made finding employment near impossible.

"Wed," said Terra pointing at the freezer.

"I respect a woman who knows what she likes," said Tom and opened the door. He riffled through the box of popsicles. He pushed his thick glasses up his nose.

"It looks like only blue and purple."

"No. Wed," said the three-year-old stamping a foot.

Tom displayed the box where she could see it. "Look, there's no red in here, but—"

Terra shrieked and stamped in place.

"Hey, hey, I think we can work this out," said Tom, leaning down and laying a hand on her shoulder.

"Want wed posicle! Wed!" said Terra, with a breathless wail.

"I wasn't dying to cook lunch anyway. We'll go for a walk through the paaark," said Tom.

The final word caught Terra's attention, and she

halted her tantrum. A single tear stalled in its pilgrimage down her dimpled cheek.

"We'll go for lunch at Hy-Vee," said Tom, "pick up some popsicles, and stop off at the park on the way home."

"Sings?" asked Terra, her hand now reaching for his.

"You drive a hard bargain," he replied. "Why not? We can't stay all afternoon because mommy will want to see you when she gets home, but we can schedule some swing time."

Terra wiped the tear from her cheek and toddled back into the living room, returning with a pair of black high-tops. She pushed them into Tom's hand and sat down on the stained boards. He shimmied each shoe onto her wiggling feet and drew the Velcro into position.

"We have to put on our coats or mommy will be mad," said Tom. He glanced into the other room to see if Susan had picked up her magical notepad to record this act of good parenting, but she was playing on her phone.

Terra looked skeptical, but after a few seconds, she skipped into the other room and returned with her hot pink jacket. Tom worked her arms through each hole and collected his own hooded windbreaker from the kitchen chair where he'd draped it. He examined himself in the mirror. He lifted his collar and adjusted his turtleneck over the scars which formed a pronounced, jagged ridge across his throat.

Susan got to her feet without looking at the pair, her clean, fur-lined coat in her arms. Moments later, the door slammed behind them.

As the three made their way first past ranch-style homes then coffeehouses and strip malls, Terra ran a few feet ahead, like a little kite bobbing happily in the wind.

Even here in Des Moines, the sky seemed to multiply endlessly in all directions, a cerulean scroll that continued to unfurl as Tom listened to the asynchronous rhythm of their steps on the pavement. In a sermon, Rain once said he settled Good Weather in Iowa because the landscape was a constant reminder of the essential link to *Shamayim*. This celestial firmament invited any seeker to tread straight through the horizon and pass peacefully on a cirrus into the next world.

Tom realized now that Rain's geographical decision probably had more to do with the low price of non-arable land during the 1990's. That's the kind of helpful disillusionment his Monday-Wednesday-Friday, two-hour therapy sessions provided, this voice in the back of his mind which sniped at his certitude with expert marksmanship. Dr. Watson's soprano cadence echoed behind every thought: *Do you think that's true? Are there any other reasons Rain might have done that? Remember sometimes the simplest explanations are closer to the truth. Occam's razor.*

Doctor Tina Watson never mentioned (or considered) that two things could be true at the same time. Negative capability fell outside her wheelhouse. But this woman half his age clearly desired to help; she wanted a better life for him. Or at least a life for him. Why? Because he was her prize case, her sole notorious cult mastermind? He never read that vibe from her. But, even in this, the doubtful voice plied its venomous trade.

Therapy kept Anna happy, which allowed him to treat Terra to popsicles and swings. Each time Terra greeted her playtime with such wild abandon, Tom felt love coursing through him like an electrical current.

Once they reached the gates to Robert Ray Family Park, Terra could no longer contain herself. She broke into a breathless sprint for the swing set.

"Remember, we can't stay too long, or these popsicles are going to turn to puddles," he called after her. But she was a prisoner to her own joy as she dashed toward the sandlot.

Tom took a seat on the bench a few yards away, his grocery bag beside him. As he watched, she kicked her tiny piston legs. Her focused expression gave way to a smile as she picked up a comfortable momentum. Tom pulled his hood further over his head and unlocked his phone.

Text from Anna: *Don't forget dinner tonight at Cosi. Sitter arrives at 6. Out the door by then.*

His fingers bumbled slowly over the keys. He had to adjust his glasses to recall where particular letters were. *Got it*, he replied. Anna had demonstrated how to set a timed reminder for himself, but he stared helplessly at the screen for a moment. After several minutes of flipping through one app then another, he gave up, uncapped a pen, and wrote on his hand. He noted Susan, his cold familiar, a few benches away then turned his attention back to Terra.

She had stalled and was talking with a blonde boy around her age. Something the boy said caused her to clutch at the chains of the swing. Then the boy extended his arms and violently shook her. Terra fell out of the swing. Her head came within inches of striking a metal pole.

"*Ben 'avah marduwth!*" swore Tom as he jumped up from the bench and raced toward his granddaughter.

A handful of other parents had already begun to gather. The blonde boy's mother, a butch woman in her thirties, pulled him back and sank to one knee.

"What were you thinking? Is that how we get what we want?"

"She was hogging," replied the blonde boy.

Tom reached the sandlot, and Terra hopped into her grandfather's arms. All thirty pounds of his granddaughter quivered. He inspected her head. She looked fine.

"Is she OK?" said the mother.

"She's not hurt," said Tom without returning the woman's concerned gaze.

"Zachary, you need to say you're sorry to..." The woman looked to Tom to supply a name.

"She's Terra. We need to leave anyway."

"Can you quickly tell Terra you're sorry?"

The blonde boy bit his lip, his eyes filling with tears. "Sawee," the blonde boy said.

A petite woman wearing a vintage Star Wars t-shirt, her long fingernails painted violet, sauntered toward the swings as Tom was turning to take his granddaughter home. Terra embedded her fingers in his jacket, and his hood softly tumbled backward.

"What's going on, babe?" asked the woman.

"We have it sorted out. Zachary apologized to Terra. She has to go, but we plan to be much nicer next time we see her, don't we?" replied the mother.

"Oh shit. You realize who that is, right? It's the guy from the documentary...Ohio or whatever. Our own local cultist extraordinaire."

With his free hand, Tom fought, fruitlessly, to put his hood up.

"No putting the cat back in the bag now. I heard that you were living around here. It's nuts that anyone could do what you did and walk free," said the mother's partner, stepping closer to Tom.

"'ome," said Terra, pointing frantically in the direction of the apartment.

Parents flocked to the periphery of the swings. A few began rounding up their children while keeping their eyes locked on Tom and the petite woman. Susan hurried toward them. Her notepad was out, and she was attempting to write as she strode.

"You're freaking everyone out," the mother said softly to her partner.

"I'm doing a public service," the angry young woman announced. She pointed a long, painted nail at Tom. "I don't want to speak for anyone else, but I don't like some psychopath hanging around our kids."

A few murmured their approval in the growing crowd.

Tom had taken a few paces away from the couple when the woman shouted, "We know what you did, big guy. What kind of sick asshole drugs all his friends then brainwashes them into offing each other? Did you get off on it? On killing your wife?"

"'ooooome," cried Terra helplessly.

Don't do it, he thought. But as though disembodied, Tom watched himself turn and draw closer to the swing set, Terra still clutched in his arms.

"Guess what, lady? Maybe not everything you see on T.V. is real life. I didn't drug anyone, and I didn't kill anyone."

The mother's partner laughed and gave him a thumbs-down.

"Maybe," said Tom, now shouting, "just maybe, things are a little more complicated than some director can wrap up in a forty-five minute episode. But, hey, if you wanna consume trash, that's not my problem. Just don't be surprised if you get worms."

"Ya done?" said the woman who had stepped in front of her partner.

"No, I'm not done. You know Dodson, that cop in the documentary, was suspended just a few days after that episode aired, right? The guy was a crackpot!"

Tom took a step toward the butch woman, hoping to explain himself. Several parents pulled their kids away.

"Tom," said Susan in a firm voice. He turned to face her. She shook her head in resignation.

"How about you back up, Charlie Manson?" said the petite woman, her hand on her phone.

Terra wept wordlessly into his shoulder. Susan, her body a taut wire, appeared on the edge of intervention.

The gathered crowd booed him as Tom carried Terra away from the park.

"Sell your bullshit somewhere else," shouted the partner, "because we ain't buying."

After traveling a few blocks, Terra still nestled in his shoulder, Tom had a realization: he had left the grocery sack with its cargo of popsicles on the park bench.

He gritted his teeth and peered up at the sky which now seemed horribly confining.

CHAPTER 3

By the time they arrived back at the apartment, the three-year-old snored on Tom's shoulder. He laid down gingerly on the couch, resting his granddaughter beside him.

"You should call Dr. Watson," chimed Susan as she shut the door behind them.

"I thought you were under strict orders to observe only," he replied.

Susan shrugged, retook her chair, and dug out her phone. She could message whoever she liked; he didn't care. Sleep weighed too heavily on him.

No psychiatrist, no survivor's group could truly understand how fatiguing it was to be the subject of so much hatred. It was like a lead vest from the dentist's office, but rather than protecting him, it only held him down. Some days, he fought to pull back the covers and put each foot onto the splintered, wood floor of the recovery center. Without Anna and Terra, he wasn't sure he'd bother. Tom closed his eyes and, with his granddaughter beside him, drifted off quickly.

"Come on," said Alle, "it's time."

It was their wedding day. As they slow-stepped toward the altar, he peered around: cousins, friends from college, but many strangers. In true Alle form, his soon-to-be wife was walking *him* down the aisle. She was giving him away to herself.

She had refused to consider some lacy gown with flowing train. No, Alle was all about the unexpected. She'd purchased this dress from the mall and adorned it with miles of gold fringe from a thrift shop.

Now she peered over at Tom and winked.

They reached the altar and stood across from one another. The ceremony began, but Tom couldn't hear the pastor's words over the volume of his own thoughts. *Don't lock your knees. You're about to sign on the deal of a lifetime.*

"The bride and groom have prepared their own vows to exchange," said the pastor. Tom remained an immobile bas relief. The pastor coughed.

"Hey, dingbat," whispered Alle, "it's time."

Some in the crowd chuckled. Tom fished in the pocket of his tuxedo for his notes. His sweaty fingers floundered in the suit. But what he took out was a bean hook, its blade sharpened to a fine edge.

"Come on," said Alle. He realized that she had her own serrated hook a breath away from his throat.

"Let's cross over together," she said. And, now, the church was gone. Around them torches blazed. Other couples, people he knew intimately, with whom he'd cleaned cabins, sung hymns, handed out Weather Forecast pamphlets in dive bars and outside strip clubs, lay in pools of blood on the camp soccer field.

In front of them was Rain. His bald head glinted in the torchlight like a coin. He wore a black robe from which his metal leg protruded. He approached Tom and with a single finger smeared an ashen mark down Tom's nose. The last rainfall. He drew his finger down Alle's nose. Suddenly, she was naked.

"Bring that to my throat," she said.

Now, Tom could see clearly that all of them were in the decayed remains of some giant animal. Maybe a whale. The torches burned atop each spire of the ribcage. Around them, the night seemed to soundlessly respirate.

"Tom," said Alle, raising his hand gripping the blade to her throat. "Come on, it's time." There was a burst of red then darkness.

Tom woke with a start. *Terra*, he remembered. He peered about frantically. But the little girl perched in front of the television. An episode of Daniel Tiger played. Prince Wednesday was learning to use the potty.

Anna sat at the foot of the couch, still sporting her heels from work. She was tucking her dark hair back into a ponytail and gripped a hair tie on her wrist.

Anna said, "You were both asleep when I got home. Susan was keeping an eye out. She left after I arrived."

"Sorry," said Tom.

"Don't have to be. But you'll owe me an actual apology if you're not ready to go in twenty. Babysitter texted me that she's on her way."

"I'll change real quick," replied Tom, glancing at the time to take note of it. He had no desire to owe any more apologies than he already did.

Thirteen minutes later, Tom emerged from her bedroom. Anna was fastening her second earring.

"Can you make sure the pedialytes are out on the counter and visible? I don't hire this girl for her brains," said Anna.

While he rustled in the cupboards, Tom heard the door open and the exchange of pleasantries. He stuck his head out.

"Hi, Jessica," he said to the young woman standing awkwardly in the foyer.

"Hi," said Jessica. She glanced at him then reached into her purse for her phone.

No doubt someone told her about Tom Duncan. An older kid, maybe even a parent. She'd probably snooped through Anna's room to find artifacts to show off. He was sure the anticipation had been thrilling, even if the payoff wasn't.

"We'll be back by 8:30," said Anna, hustling Tom toward the door. "If anything comes up, you have my cell, and the restaurant is just a few blocks down."

Jessica raised two fingers in acknowledgement but avoided locking eyes with either of them. Terra remained preoccupied with PBS. Before shutting the door, Tom noted that Daniel Tiger was finally getting his crack at potty time.

Anna had been hesitant to establish any permanent ties with her returned father, but dinner at Cosi had become something of a routine. Anna enjoyed the Moscow mules and calamari. Tom appreciated the dim ambience. A luminous hearth burned in every season and scattered hanging bulbs illuminated each table. But between these fixtures, darkness held dominion, and the odds of being recognized were low.

"How was work?" asked Tom as he brought an olive oil dipped roll toward his mouth.

Anna shrugged and took a sip of her mule, considering the question.

"I don't know what I was thinking hiring Kristine. Have you ever heard anyone with a nasally Tennessee accent?"

"I had no idea such a linguistic monstrosity was possible," replied Tom.

"I wouldn't have thought so either. Think Sandra Bullock in *The Blindside*, but Sandra is wheezing through every line. And she wants to talk about refinancing your mortgage."

Tom began to laugh and had to cover his mouth to keep from coughing up the bread.

"Nothing puts me," said Tom, struggling to keep a straight face, "in a buying mood like heavy-breathing in an unintelligible accent. It's why my worst nightmare is a congested Count Dracula calling to extend my car's warranty."

The punchline landed just as he hoped, and Anna attempted to hide a smile. But the effort was futile.

"Okay, okay," she said. "You can't make me laugh. You just can't. I need to share some things, and I need to start now before I lose my nerve."

She took a deep breath. A surge of ice poured through Tom's veins.

"Sure, okay," he replied.

"I've rehearsed a thousand ways to tell you this. Every one of them hurts when I've played it through in my mind, so I think just need to be direct: I don't think you can live near us. We need you to not be around, at least for a while."

His leg bounced anxiously under the table. He weighed one thought then another, like a janitor trying keys on a ring, but couldn't move his lips to begin.

"I guess...I hoped...since I've been doing the sessions—" he said.

"I appreciate you getting help. I do."

"Then...it's about Terra. Is it because I fell asleep earlier? I keep her safe, I don't let her run too far ahead on the walks, sometimes I do have to pull her back. I mean, I can keep a closer eye—"

"It's not that. If she's in any danger, honestly, and I don't relish saying this, it's because she's with you."

"That's not fair," said Tom.

"Dad, look at me," said Anna. He stared into his wife's eyes in his daughter's face.

"People are angry at you. I have seen the way complete strangers approach you. And, look, I really in my heart of hearts believe you were a victim. But plenty of people don't. My coworkers stop talking when I enter the breakroom. I'm a pariah. Life was hard before you came home. Now, it's harder. Jessica's mother wasn't even going to let her past our doorway before I talked her down."

"Do these people have no conception of what 'dropped all charges' means?" Tom whispered through gritted teeth.

"Terra deserves to grow up feeling like she can go to the park without a crowd forming to watch her grandfather's screaming match with a stranger," replied Anna.

She leaned back. This was her big reveal. And suddenly, Tom realized how worn she looked. Tom ran his hands along the cracks in the colorful, glossed table. He'd never noticed how sorry the finish was.

"That isn't what went down. Did Susan break her vow of silence to sling that bullshit?" he asked.

"Doesn't matter. And even if the park never happened, we'd still be having this conversation because I had to buy new curtains to keep out cameramen. I had to ask Mrs. Livitz to install new locks on the entryway doors. I—"

"I get it," said Tom. "But what if I just don't leave the apartment with Terra? What if we just stay in when I'm over?"

"It's not enough right now. I've asked Aunt Stella to come back and help for a little while. She's retired, and we have the room. Terra loves you, and I want you to be a part of her life. But this is for you too. Your scars may have healed, but you're depressed and pissed off all the time. You need time to process too."

"I'm in control of myself," replied Tom.

"Ok, then tell me you intended to yell at that woman in the park," said Anna. Tom rubbed at his throat. He remained silent. He didn't know how to answer that.

"This isn't forever. I want you to come home once you let some of this go. But Dr. Watson and I agreed," Anna continued.

"I'm glad Dr. Watson was part of the conversation. Makes me feel like a lab rat."

"It isn't just that," said Anna abruptly. "Katie Hunt called me. Her name at Good Weather was Thames, right?"

Tom let the words wash over him. At another table to

their right, two parents chatted. Their son played on a handheld console, while their daughter unwrapped and rewrapped her silverware.

"Why did Thames call you?"

"She didn't know how to reach you, but I guess she remembered my name. She must have looked me up through my work directory. She asked me to tell you that the other former Good Weather members, people who were gone during the suicide, are having a remembrance ceremony. It's this weekend. They reserved a block of rooms at the Holiday Inn west of Edenburg. I think calling me was her last ditch effort to find you."

Tom regretted putting anything in his stomach. An urge to vomit pressed on him like a weighty barbell.

"You want to see them, don't you?" said Anna.

"Of course not."

"Dr. Watson doesn't want you anywhere near Edenburg, and neither do I," said Anna.

"I said that I don't want to go."

"And I'm saying that I don't believe you," she replied. Anna remained still as a snake. "I can't stop you. It's your decision. You're a grown adult after all. Whatever you decide, honestly, don't tell me. It's none of my business. I'm telling you to leave, but I can't tell you where not to go."

Tom winced as though he'd been given a shot.

"Understand this isn't easy for me. I want Terra to make memories with her grandfather. I want her to fall asleep with you on the couch. But I can't be afraid all the time that your old life will come back to haunt you or that you'll lose control on one of these people and they will hurt you or Terra..." said Anna.

Steaming fettuccini arrived for the neighboring table. The daughter bounced her fork eagerly in her palm. The mother folded a napkin over her son's lap.

"Can I at least have tomorrow morning to say goodbye?"

"I think that would be fine," replied Anna. "Aunt Stella won't be here by then."

"I don't think I can eat," said Tom. "Can we just leave a twenty and go home?"

"Yeah," replied Anna, her voice solemn and quiet. "That'll work for now."

CHAPTER 4

Tom let his legs dangle over the front of his rusted out 2003 Hyundai Sonata and took another swig of his PBR. Surely no one loved the taste of this beer. After all, no one raved about Saltines or iceberg lettuce. The only good thing about PBR was that it conjured the hundreds of other nights he'd downed a can. It was nostalgia in an aluminum case.

In the station parking lot, a hooded teen tightened his gas cap. He hopped in the GT as other teens spoke animatedly from the back seat. They peeled away. What remained was the fluorescent glitter off the pumps and the faint smell of oil.

These, the sights and smells of Iowa at night, were Tom's true memory serum. The PBR was mostly for show.

As he watched, a middle-aged woman with shoulder-length brown hair emerged from the gas station and approached his lookout. She wore boot cut jeans and a loose flannel shirt. She had opted to go shoeless and passed the pumps without gazing at anything but him.

"Nice night for a walk," he said. "Not sure I would have

forgone shoes, Alle."

"Once you've done it enough, your soles toughen up," she replied and hoisted herself to join him in his perch on the hood. "And what are we if not tough souls?"

"You've made me tougher than I'd like. I wish I had the energy to scream at you," said Tom.

"Since I'm just the me you want to talk to, the version you loved, the one you could stomach to see, I'm not sure there's much purpose."

"So even if I spit on you? Curse you?"

"It'd be cathartic for a second. But I'm not the version of Alle that has it coming, I'm afraid."

Tom looked down, nodding in resignation.

"Our daughter is kicking me out of her life."

"She's scared," replied Alle and laid her head on his shoulder. "She's scared for Terra and for you."

"I know. And I doubt she'd be comforted to learn that I'm out here conversing with ghosts."

"Fair. But I think, if you really consider it, you're even more afraid than she is. Maybe that's why you're chatting with me, your friendly neighborhood phantasm."

Alle nuzzled closer and looped an arm around his.

"That night...I was willing to throw everything away because I knew there would be no tomorrow with you in it. Terra, she would have just been a name someone said once. I would never have known her..."

"If you'd gone on with the rest of us," she finished.

Tom rose from the car and took another drink of beer.

"I don't know where you've gone. Or Rain or Atlantic or anyone. And now Anna and Terra are floating down a different branch without me. I've survived just to lose them anyway."

"You're being dramatic," replied Alle. She assumed a cross-legged pose on the hood of the car, her arms folded in her lap like an idol.

"I didn't crest the falls at the end of the world, but I should have, because all the living want to talk about is the dead."

"I'm just an ethereal being made manifest by your psyche, but if I might interject," said Alle, raising a finger in protest. "You can always change the conversation. You're still here: blood and bones and spirit."

Alle approached him and laid her hands on his chest.

"All that means is I can still be hurt," Tom replied. "What do I do?"

"You go to Edenburg. Even if you want to move on, the dreams, the memories, me, it's all you think about. You want to go, and there's nothing for you here right now. Anna said as much. They'll be plenty of time to come back and wait for Anna to reopen the door. People just need to forget you."

"I'm forever at the mercy of every binge-watching know-nothing with two working eyes and an urge to run their mouth. People like that have nothing better to do than remember," Tom said, draining the last of his beer.

"You'd be surprised how quickly people forget. For example, I definitely never wore boot cut jeans. Too country chic. I was a straight-leg lady."

"Now I'm losing you too, huh?" said Tom.

"Just the bits that don't matter. Someday, you'll try to remember my face and just see water, opaque and formless. That's how every good thing goes."

"I don't think I could live with that," Tom replied. The wind cracked and spun with the sound of a passing car in the distance.

"'Out on Red Road the traffic continues. Everything continues. Nor does memory sleep. It goes on,'" said Alle.

Tom ruffled through the paper bag, took out a new PBR, popped the tab, and drank.

"I am pretty sure you didn't read Donald Justice," he said. "I'm filling in the blanks already."

Alle shrugged. She walked back toward the gas station.

"Tell everyone left I said hello. Especially Thames. I think she might need to hear it."

"I didn't say I'd go. And I haven't forgiven you," Tom called after her. But when he blinked, Alle was gone. In the dimly-lit gas station, the attendant held a hand to the glass and peered in his direction.

Tom chugged the last of his PBR and felt in his pocket for his keys. He popped a salute to the attendant.

When Terra stumbled sleepily from her room the next morning, Tom sat in the kitchen with Susan. Terra took his hand and led him to the cupboard in the kitchen where the Cinnamon Toast Crunch was kept.

Tom watched her put away spoonfuls doused in milk. She hummed and thumped her feet lightly on the table's supports. He wondered if this was how renowned painters felt as they watched their greatest masterpiece unfold before them. He was enchanted. Afterward, she placed him on the couch, raced into her room, and returned with her copy of *Edward the Cat*. She ran her hands across each illustration as he read, outlining the kittens with her index finger.

After two complete readings, they turned on Disney+ and let *The Aristocats* play. Terra cuddled in beside him with her stuffed horse. When the movie came to an end, she turned her head to look at him. He hit "play again." And, in what felt like only a few minutes to Tom, the afternoon was an iridescent memory.

When the second showing came to an end, he prepped boiling water for spaghetti and spooned a can of sauce into a microwave-safe bowl, added extra garlic, just like the girls liked.

Anna arrived home, and they ate around the table together. It was quieter than usual, but the house was warm from the oven where Tom had baked garlic bread. They all seemed to be content, bobbing along in the kindness of this moment.

After dinner, Tom got in his car. It took a few tries, but it started. Terra sat in her mom's arms and waved as he put the Sonata into gear. While Tom watched through the rearview, Terra rubbed her eyes, and Anna carried her inside. There would be time for another reading of *Edward the Cat*, maybe a cartoon or two. Then the only two people he loved on this whole planet would be asleep hundreds of miles away from him, and, though he was loathe to admit it, safer for it.

CHAPTER 5

From the Netflix Documentary Series *The Good Weather* "Episode 1: A Tempest in the Heartland"

(The scene opens with a slow-focus shot on a color photograph of a young man in uniform. His face is ruddy and spotted with acne. He grins with pride. Director Don Burlington narrates as the camera focuses in on the images.)

Burlington: "Leonard Fairbanks, who the world would come to know as 'Rain,' leader of the Good Weather cult, tried his hand at more than one trade before he began recruiting followers in Iowa City.

"In the summer of 1991, after a night of heavy drinking, Fairbanks enlisted in the army at a recruiting station in Rochester, Illinois. He was deemed fit for service and shipped off to Fort Hood. Fairbanks spent several weeks in Texas. But after suffering an accident in a munitions bunker during basic training, he was subsequently discharged. The accident cost him his right leg. He told friends that he lost the limb in a firefight in The Gulf War and that, as a member of black ops operating in Iran, his records had been classified.

"Fairbanks returned home to Yeoman, Illinois in early winter of 1991. According to acquaintances, he took up novel writing while he adapted to his prosthetic leg. Over the course of several months, he wrote a western called *Last Star of the Alamo*. Fairbanks refused to let family or friends read the book, claiming it was 'the pinnacle of genius.' Fairbanks sent the manuscript to several New York agents."

(A bespectacled woman who a caption identifies as "Lisa Suskins, Former Literary Agent for Parker & Row" speaks to the camera.)

Suskins: "You might expect that someone with that loose of a grip on reality would not have much of a gift for realistic fiction. But the manuscript he sent was promising, I'll admit. The main character was a Yiddish cowboy, and Fairbanks clearly did his homework to get the Hebrew right. It had shootouts, stampedes, a lady in distress. It wasn't a page turner, but it was good genre work."

(The documentary cuts to an image of the manuscript. A hand-drawn cowboy, shirtless, sporting a necklace adorned with the Star of David cracks a whip as Mexican soldiers on horseback approach.)

"But the love story was hokey. And you can't sell a Western with a crap love story. It was clear Fairbanks didn't have a clue how to write intimate dialogue, and, in my experience, you can't fake that.

"I don't have the exact date written down, but in March, I called to tell him it just wasn't gonna happen with the book in its current form. I had a freelance editor I wanted to refer him to in Bloomington. But after I told him we weren't accepting the book, he went nuts. Leonard just started screaming into the phone that I didn't know anything, and that, hell or high water, it was scripture's will that the book get published." (She laughs) "Someone, I think his mother, tried to pull him off the line, and I could hear her shouting to calm down, that he was ruining his big shot.

"He started cursing. Then the line just went dead. As you can imagine, I wasn't keen to call back. Word got out once I talked to my boss, and no one wanted to work with him after that."

(The documentary cuts to a fly-over of rural Illinois. White birds flap in slow formation over the landscape. Barns and farmhouses blemish massive expanses of tawny fields.)

Burlington: "In June of 1992, running short on money, Fairbanks began making the rounds in the local Baptist churches in Rochester. He requested donations for a supposed youth ministry and center for homeless veterans in Iowa City. The local populace of Rochester, whose politics and faith were at odds with the college town, were happy to send Fairbanks on his mission. He was strange, one pastor noted in a letter to another, but he was still a champion of rural, Christian values."

(The documentary shows an image of a street in Iowa City where co-eds pass on a brick sidewalk. A homeless man sleeps on a bench nearby. In front of him is an open guitar case for change.)

"In August of 1992, Fairbanks signed a lease for a property on Johnson Street and founded The Good Weather Congregation. Within a week, Fairbanks won his first two converts: Lisa Duncan (later known as 'Alle') and Katie Hunt (later known as 'Thames')."

(The documentary cuts to a scruffy man who a caption identifies as "Greg, local resident.")

Greg: "We'd see Leonard out on the corner holdin' up signs and shouting, 'Have you made peace with your maker? The end is near!' All that kinda stuff. People mostly just crossed the street or laughed at him.

"But then he gets these two pretty gals—Tom Duncan's wife and Katie Hunt who tended bar over at Raccoon Saloon—and people actually knew them. We liked them. Lisa, Tom's wife, taught school kids, and the parents loved her. Anyway, I think those two, they probably ganged up on him, got him to dial it back a bit. A touch less fire-and-brimstone. And pretty soon, Saturday night service over at Good Weather was growin'. They were handing out pamphlets, chatting up kids on campus.

"And you could figure out who was really," (Gary imitates a fish with a hook in its mouth) "because they made you call 'em something fuckin' weird."

(The documentary cuts to a short Latina woman in her fifties. Her hair is cropped close to her head; she exudes the energy of someone half her age. A caption identifies her as "Elise Hernandez, 'Rio,' Good Weather member 1992-2015.")

Rio: "How'd they convince me? I joined up because I'd lived my whole life on the outside. I didn't conform to heteronormative, white, small town Iowa. The people at Good Weather didn't care. They were all outsiders like me.

"Most Saturdays, we'd go out to English River and baptize people who had committed. In the early days, there were always a few. Sometimes a full van. Katie would drive because while we were cruising down I-80, Rain would point at each one of the newbies and say a body of water. And that became their name. So, if he said," (pointing at the camera) "'You're Michigan,' well, that's all anyone would call you. I was from Texas, so I was 'Rio' for 'Rio Grande.' The newbies thought it was a joke at first. But then they'd look over at Lisa and Katie, who weren't laughing at all; they were dead-serious when it came to Rain. And the names stuck."

(The camera cuts to an open Hebrew Bible.)

Burlington: "Reappellation, an act which Rain compared to Adam naming all the creatures of the earth, was just one tenet of the budding spiritual community."

(The documentary cuts back to Rio.)

Rio: "When Rain talked about heaven, he called it *Shamayim*. It's Hebrew, means 'two waters.' Rain loved that kind of stuff. He used to go to synagogue as a kid even though he wasn't Jewish. If you wanted to be a part of what was going on at Good Weather, you had to learn some Hebrew. *Nephesh*," (Rio pats her throat) "that's your spirit, and in Good Weather theology, it lives here. Anyone who didn't believe, they're *Rasha*. Wicked, wicked ones. You could say that if someone said something nasty to you while you were out at the Ped Mall handing out pamphlets. It was a good way to vent."

(An audio recording of Rain plays. The documentary captions his quick, fluid speech.)

Rain: "Ohio, is that thing on?" (Muffled chatter) "Because I got big news. Oh, I got good news, y'all." (Scattered cheers) "That all you got? You gonna wish you cheered louder once you hear what I'm tellin' you. Let me hear it again." (Loud cheering)

"Last night, I'm layin' in my bed. Cows are out in the field mooing. I got my leg on the nightstand." (Sound of

Rain tapping his metal leg then laughter) "And I'm praying, 'Oh true scripture, let me hear you. True scripture, let me hear you.' I don't know why this was on my mind, but I felt some spirit pulling me.

"Then there's this voice, real soft. It's calling me from the other room. You know how gentle it is when rain is just pattering on the window? That quiet. The voice says, 'Rain the prophet, get up. Put on a pot of coffee. I got something to show you.' So, I'm excited, but I'm terrified."

('What did you do?' comes a voice from the congregation.)

"Well, I got the hell up! Whaddya think!" (Laugher, scattered applause) "And when I walk into the kitchen, there's a being already sittin' there. Its clothes are radiant, but they were floating over her like water. I said 'Are you an angel of the true scripture? A *Malak*?'

"She says 'Sit down, Rain.' And she pushes the chair toward me. In front of it, there's this notebook and a pen. There's a flowerpot, full of black-eyed Susans, that I'd picked a week ago. Only now, it looks like they were just plucked. And they're in full bloom.

"So, I sit. She says, 'Write,' and as soon as the pen is in my hand she just starts talking. And I know every word matters, so I'm putting it down a mile-a-minute. And time, while I was writing, it felt like it slowed down. You know how when you're underwater, if you open your eyes, everything looks out of sync? It was like that. I feel like I been writing the last two years, but I wasn't hungry or thirsty. When I was writing, I was fed by the Spirit. Like Elijah. I passed to *Shamayim* for a season and came back. Some of you, I don't even recognize. I'm serious.

"Thames found me passed out this morning, pen still

in my hand. And she said I was still glowing, and my skin was clammy like I'd been deep sea diving." ('What'd she tell you? The *Malak?*' someone shouts.)

"Now, now I'm getting' to that. You gotta give me a minute. As you can imagine, I'm still a little weary. And it's gonna take time to transcribe all the new scripture in a way that makes sense because, make no mistake, that is what she gave me, new scripture. But I rushed over here because I want to give you the bottom line: the world is gonna wash away." (Clapping) "The old faiths, the old creeds? They ain't gonna save you. But the true scripture? What we're doing here? That's your life raft." (Cheers and praises)

"All those people you knew before you set off toward *Shamayim* here with me, with us, all that flotsam you were clinging to—booze or drugs or sex—you need to dump that off quick because it's sink or swim time. A big storm is brewin'. The people treading the old ways, sitting dead-eyed in the pews, walkin' the walk on Sundays then going out and drowning in the darkness of this world? They're going down, too. The storm is coming, and it ain't Fujita scale six. Not ten. It's going to be one hundred, y'all.

"And right here, this family, this faith," (a loud sound of Rain slapping a podium) "it's your ark. I don't want a single one of you to burn because scripture is clear: the second death is all flame and endless, restless wind tearing you apart. And if you turn your back and walk away, there's not a shelter in the world that can withstand what's coming. Only the true scripture can do that."

(The documentary cuts back to Rio.)

Rio: "How did we feel when he told us that?"

Interviewer: "Yeah."

Rio: "I was happy. Elated. Over the moon."

Interviewer: "You were happy that everyone else was going to burn?"

Rio: "Totally. My mom and my stepdad were methhead losers. They couldn't care less about me. I moved out of the trailer when I was fourteen. Everyone I went to school with called me a fag.

"When Rain told me they'd been wrong about me, that every school counselor, every social worker had it backwards, that they were worthless and were gonna burn, not me, you better believe I was thrilled. I figured, 'Screw them. Everyone I love is sitting right here in this room.'

"That was Rain's whole thing. He made you feel like you were the only person on the planet. Like the roof could cave in and crush you to nothing, and if you were sitting there with him, all was well."

(The documentary cuts to a group photo of The Good Weather community. They fill the entire frame, almost two hundred people, mostly young. In the center, Rain, his head completely shaved and dressed in black robes, stands with Thames and Alle on either side. Ohio is kissing Alle on the cheek, and she smiles broadly.)

Burlington: "In late spring of 1993, Rain encouraged members to sever ties with their families and to turn over all financial resources to the church. Rain also began directly cashing the paychecks of members. This caught the attention of federal and state officials. Facing pressure, by nearly unanimous consensus, the Baptist Conference of Eastern Iowa cut funding to the Good Weather congregation and excommunicated all members."

(Footage of flickering flames plays.)

"Public sentiment turned against the community as

they became more insular and disconnected. In June, vandals spray-painted pentagrams on the narthex windows. Police opened an investigation, but the officer in charge took little action. Then, in early July, a masked assailant threw a Molotov cocktail through the main door to the church during a Sunday service. Tom Duncan was able to quickly extinguish the blaze. But the message was clear. The Good Weather community wasn't welcome in Iowa City."

(The documentary switches to a snapshot of the cover of *Forbes*, February 1990. A young black man with well-defined features and a robust hairline adorns the cover. His arms are crossed in defiance. The copy reads: "Gerald Benson: The Seed King of Iowa.")

"Fortunately for the cult, some months earlier, Thames and Rain befriended Gerald Benson, the millionaire owner of Benson Seed Supply. In early June, Benson was reppellated 'Atlantic' and began bankrolling the congregation's endeavors. At Rain's behest, Benson negotiated the purchase of Shine or Rain Summer Camp outside of Edenburg, Iowa. The deal was finalized in August, and by early September, the property on Johnson Street was vacant."

(The documentary cuts back to Greg.)

Greg: "They rented this bus to pack up all their shit. Once it was gone, to be honest, everyone was relieved. Like you'd hear people at the bar shouting about how 'The circus finally left town!' It was good to laugh about it, but we all knew someone who got caught up and left with 'em.

"Every fall, I'd see flocks of freshman moving around campus. And the Good Weather people would be back, just standing around, waiting for one or another of them students to start walking back to the dorm by themselves. They were pure predators.

"You can't keep kids safe with people like that around. Kids want to drink themselves sick? Sure. They want to smoke reefer on the square? I ain't gonna partake, but be my guest. But you gotta have some guardrails. You can't let these teens far from home get into sucked into this cult shit. Once they go down, they never come up for air. And, well, some of 'em didn't. And we gotta live with that. That's the sad truth."

CHAPTER 6

Tom Duncan's phone sat snuggly in the Sonata's cupholder and refused to ding. He watched for any illumination that would indicate a text message. He keened his ears for the slightest sound of vibration, but the phone remained stubbornly silent.

Some hours before, he texted Anna. He had measured the heft of each message in his mind, placing it on some psychic balance, before recognizing the error of it. Finally, he'd settled on *Left Des Moines. Hope to come home soon. Miss you both.*

Tom piloted the vehicle around a curve. Below, the land sloped under a genial, emerging sunlight. The hills were rugged by Iowa standards, and an incautious driver could find himself skidding down one of these talus-littered shoulders. But, for Tom, this was familiar turf.

Tom lifted the phone to his field of vision. Full bars. No messages. He replaced it in the cupholder.

For the last few hours, he'd been mentally preparing himself for Edenburg. Who else would want to run their fingers along old scars like this? If Thames had been able to track him down, surely she'd invited everyone. But there weren't many Good Weathers left. They could fill an Overlook-size ballroom with ghosts, but the living were few.

But what if local or, or worse, national press got wind of the reunion? The prospect of rehashing his practiced responses to the press's inquiries—"What did you email Lindsey Stenson?" "Why did you kill your friends?" "Do you regret it?"—made him feel like a scarecrow gutted with a pitchfork.

Tom's hand tightened reflexively on the wheel.

He had heard the editors of the documentary cut together footage to create the perception that he knew Lindsey Stenson well. It was good story-telling; he had to give them that. But the truth was he couldn't be sure he'd said two words to the woman. His most vivid memory of Lindsey was a fuzzy recollection of her stationed atop the pitching mound during a community softball game. She'd played college ball, a year or two, and he struck out swinging. Her arms were unusually thin and spindly. He'd wondered how she could chuck a ball that fast with those spaghetti strands. He'd been impressed. That was a few years before she left and totally changed her life. What blackmail Rain had on her, to pull her back in like that, he couldn't imagine. She seemed so nice.

He glanced down at the phone. He pressed the screen with his finger to draw the machine out of sleep mode. Still nothing.

When he looked back at the road, he realized his carelessness. The Sonata sped toward the guardrails. The end of the blacktop highway rushed to meet him.

Tom pressed hard on the brake and forced the steering

wheel hard to the left. The wheels peeled out under the force of the change in direction. The Sonata jutted further than Tom intended, and an oncoming car swerved to dodge. As it passed, the car blared its horn in reproach.

Tom readjusted and shunted the car back into the right lane. He looked in the mirror, but the highway behind was empty. No danger of being rear-ended. Without taking his eyes from the road, Tom withdrew the phone from the cup holder and laid it face down on the seat. He found an oldies station on the dial and turned it loud enough to drown out all thought.

The Holiday Inn on Route 20 in Edenburg was part of a complex of two hotels, a gas station, and a casino. Tom passed through the sliding glass doors as a pair of morning travelers exited sipping coffee from Styrofoam cups. The wheels of his overnight bag clacked along the immaculately kept tile. The usual assortment of nondescript couches and chairs populated the lobby, but they appeared more pristine than usual. An impressive crystalline chandelier cast glowing orbs on the thoroughfare.

It seemed unnecessarily adorned for a hotel that Tom assumed most travelers used just to catch some winks between stretches in the casino. He approached the check-in where an attendant stared down at his monitor.

"Welcome to the Holiday Inn. Checking out?" said the attendant, donning a wide grin.

"Checking in for Tom Duncan. Any chance my room is available a little early?"

Tom placed his ID and cash on the counter. The cash was a loan, a parting gift from the Cult Recovery Center. He doubted if he would be able to repay it any time soon.

He suspected that was understood.

The attendant picked up the ID and began typing.

"Looks like we have your room ready!" he said. "Credit card for incidentals?"

Tom pulled out his nearly maxed card and handed it over. The attendant swiped it. A woman emerged from an office behind the counter. She tugged the door closed behind her and reeled her badge down to lock it.

"I can finish this," she said. "Why don't you go see what progress the cleaning crew has made on four?"

She moved toward the counter, giving Tom a perfunctory smile.

"I just need to link his door keys," replied the attendant.

"I got it," said the woman. "You tell the crew that once they're done with four, I want them to stop off at the pool and collect towels before they go to five."

"Okeydokey," replied the attendant jovially and scampered off.

The woman slid the credit card and ID back along the marble counter toward Tom. He breathed silent relief.

She scanned the door keys and placed each one in a colorful sleeve. She turned toward Tom but did not hand him the sleeve.

"Mr. Duncan, I'm Sylvia Dennis. I'm the manager here. I want to talk with you about your stay this weekend."

Her words seemed practiced with the same precision that one dices an onion.

"It's been a long drive, and I was hoping to catch some sleep before I meet my...before the reunion starts. I'm part of a group. Did I mention that?" replied Tom.

"Yes, I'm aware. That's what I'd like to talk to you

about. You likely don't remember him, but my son is
Robby Dennis."

Even in his groggy state, he instantly knew the name.

"I remember Robby," replied Tom. "He was on the
detasseling crew. Hard worker."

"Yes, he is," replied Sylvia. "His father is an EMT with
the county. And his father was one of the first on the scene
out at Shine or Rain on August 7th."

Tom set his overnight bag down. Suddenly, the
refractions from the chandelier were blindingly bright.

"His father needed counseling after what he saw. And
bear in mind, he'd driven ambulances in Chicago. What
you all did out there..." Sylvia exhaled deeply.

"And the worst part was that we'd trusted you to
employ our son. I'd told Robby he needed a summer job,
couldn't be at loose ends all day. His father blamed
me...we're still working through it."

"I'm sorry," said Tom.

Her face remained as devoid of expression as before.

"I'm a professional," she replied, "and I have never in
my twenty-four years denied service to anyone. I don't
plan to start today. But I want you to know that I thought
very hard about whether we, our community, should allow
you back." She paused for a moment, considering her
words. "Frankly if it had been me, I would have set flame
to that entire camp and let weeds take the whole. I
certainly would not have made the EMTs and forensic
teams clean up your mess."

She hadn't intended to say this last bit. Tom could tell.
The words came forth with geyser quickness.

"I see why you might feel that way," responded Tom.
"But, to be frank, I'm just one guy, and I'm not Rain."

"Oh come on," snorted Sylvia. "Man up and take a little responsibility. You know what you did."

Don't lose it. You can't afford to lose it, he heard the voice of Dr. Watson repeating. But it was too late. While he hadn't gone over the cliff earlier, now the brakes were cut.

"If you caught me on a different day when I'd slept, maybe I could muster more empathy, maybe dole out some closure. But if anything came out of Good Weather, it wasn't closure, not for me. So, if that's what you're in the market for, lady, I'd be selling you a bill of goods on an inventory I don't own."

The manager raised a finger to cut in, but before she could, Tom felt a firm grip fall on his shoulder.

"Hello, Sylvia," said Bryce Benson. He had draped one massive arm over Tom's shoulder and pulled him close.

For the first time since she had emerged from the back office, Sylvia Dennis smiled. It was a foolish, toothy grin.

"Mr. Benson, I heard you were staying with us."

"I am, and you can't imagine how much we appreciate you hosting us. This weekend is pretty emotional for everyone, especially Tom."

"Absolutely," responded Sylvia, looking slightly cowed.

"Hey, no need to be embarrassed. You and your husband lost something at that camp. I get that. I lost my dad," Benson said, his face sober but strangely friendly. "But Tom, he lost his faith, his wife, every friend he had in the world. And in the most horrible way possible."

Sylvia turned her gaze back to Tom. She appeared to be sizing him up as though sympathy were a fitted suit.

"What I mean to say is that we hear you. You and the Edenburg community are victims of what happened too," said Bryce. "And, if you feel like it, the two of us could have a drink some night and talk about how we cope with that."

"I'd love that," said Sylvia eagerly. "My husband and I, we used to drive down to Iowa City to see your games. And, my, you were just a spectacular player. We were there when you took that punt back for a touchdown against Michigan State in 2012."

"Oh," said Bryce, grinning ear to ear, "that was a game, wasn't it?" He held one arm stiffly in front of him and mimed carrying a football with his other.

"It sure was," said Sylvia. "Oh! Let me get you your key. I've completely forgotten myself."

She indecorously dropped Tom's sleeve of keys in front of him and began frenetically typing in the computer. Tom picked them up before she could change her mind and ducked away.

"Wait for me, will you?" Bryce called after him.

Tom picked a couch out of sight of the counter, and a few minutes later, Bryce Benson jogged up. He wore fitted designer jeans and a black hoodie. He had Atlantic's rugged jawline and athlete's build.

"You got old on me, Mr. Duncan," said Bryce with a laugh.

"Well, when you haven't seen someone since the age of, what, eight?" asked Tom.

"Nine, actually," replied Bryce. "My mom pulled it together enough to demand custody in '02. I remember because she took me to see *Harry Potter and the Chamber of Secrets* in theaters. It fueled my secret crush on Emma Watson for years to come."

Tom laughed.

"And Tom is just fine now. No 'Mr. Duncan,'" he said.

"No need to age me further."

The two rounded the corner and both reached for the elevator button.

"Age before beauty," said Tom and clicked it. "I admit that I'm a little surprised to see you. You were so young when you left. I don't expect you remember much of anything about Good Weather. What's brings you to this merry gathering?"

The elevator signaled its arrival, and the doors parted. Bryce extended his hands in invitation.

"Honestly, I'm here on the company dime," Bryce said once the elevator doors had closed. "Dad's connection to Good Weather is a PR liability. The board wants someone on the ground, so I agreed to chaperone. I'll be ensuring you maintain arm's length if there is any dancing and checking that no one spikes the punch.

"But the company didn't have to put a gun to my head, honestly. I loved my dad in spite of his many problems. And you all were his friends. I thought it might help if I was here."

Coming from anyone else, this statement might have seemed self-aggrandizing or insincere, but from the mouth of Byrce Benson, it was pure honey.

"Honestly," said Tom as the elevator doors parted, "it already has."

CHAPTER 7

Tom wheeled his suitcase through the entry, allowed the door to fall shut, and flopped on the bed. In his pocket, he felt his phone buzz. He pulled it out and held it inches from his eyes: *French toast for breakfast. We miss you too.*

He took off his glasses and stationed them on the nightstand. He felt he could sleep a few eons and not be overdoing it.

Don't dream of Rain. Don't dream of Rain, he prayed. He closed his eyes, picturing Terra chewing a mouth full of French toast, her blue plastic fork waving in the air like a baton. He began to think of Anna. Then he was gone.

He didn't dream of Rain. Instead, he was back in the clothing store where he'd worked as an undergrad.

It was after hours. A manager counted cash from the till. A girl whose name he couldn't place had cleaned out the fitting rooms and retrieved all the garments which customers had passed on. The employees, including Tom, gathered around the cash register where they refolded pants and pinned shirts.

There were bins upon bins to return to their rightful places in the store, and from time to time, one person or another would zip away with a stack of jeans or t-shirts in their arms. But Tom remained dutifully at his station, an acolyte of and witness to this great restoration. His hands glided in practiced patterns—a turquoise camisole, an emerald men's large dress shirt, its onyx buttons like the eyes of some benign and curious insect.

He wanted this moment to continue indefinitely, to be forever in this procession. To be integral. But the manager was reaching the terminus of her count, and one-by-one, the employees came to the end of their bins of rumpled clothes.

Soon, they'd be called to the rear of the store to collect their bags and coats from the grey industrial lockers. They'd parade in a neat column to the entry. The manager would unlock the gate, and ducking under, they'd exit the mall and muster back to their cars in the monolithic garage.

Of course, he knew in a day's time he'd be executing this same routine, perhaps even refolding the same garments, which had been rejected a second time. The manager would again be keying totals on the adding machine.

But, in this moment, he was clinging to this night, this second where if he could only maintain this synchronous commune, he'd never be alone, not really.

Then there was a loud rapping at the entryway gate. Only he appeared to notice, but he didn't dare to call out for fear of breaking their circuit. But then, the knocking again, and now others heard it too and peered up from their nearly complete task.

Tom woke with a start. He fumbled for his glasses and bumped the digital alarm to the floral-patterned carpet with a *whump.*

"If you're trying to duck me, Tom Duncan, you're doing an awful job," came a sing-song voice from the hallway.

Tom recovered his glasses, reset the fallen clock, and made his way to the door. He opened it and allowed his eyes to settle on Elise Hernandez. Rio. She wore a tall hat with a bright purple feather. A black leather jacket covered a vintage Pixies t-shirt and high-waisted jeans. Joan Jett appeared tame by comparison.

"I was actually searching for Tom Duncan's room, but I seem to have stumbled upon the entrance to a nursing home attached to this hotel," said Rio, cracking a smile. "You must forgive me, sir. I'll let you get back to your shuffleboard."

"Oh Rio, if you hadn't said something, I never would have seen you out here," replied Tom.

"Well-played, old man. Get over here."

She stepped forward and hugged Tom. He returned the gesture, but with some hesitation. He hadn't forgotten her appearance in *The Good Weather.*

She pushed the door open and stepped inside.

"I see you also did not purchase the luxury suite," she said, bouncing lightly on the bed, then assuming a reclining position. "I suppose that is reserved for one Bryce Benson."

"I'm surprised the manager didn't sign over the deed to the whole place right at check-in. She was smitten with him. Did you see him yet?"

Tom assumed the chair across from the bed. Rio

kicked her flats off.

"How do you think I found your room? We bumped into each other whilst I partook of the ice machine: just one of the amenities offered by yoooooooooour Edenburg Holiday Inn," she said stretching her arms in front of herself, presenting his room to him as though it were a gameshow prize. "How are ya, Tom? What's life these days?"

Tom considered for a moment. "Dynamic."

"Ooooo," replied Rio, "simultaneously enticing and mysterious. I like it."

"How's the state of Colorado?"

"Two words for you," she paused for effect. "Legal. Weed."

Rio maintained mock seriousness for a second then they both burst out laughing.

"So, husband, kids?" asked Tom.

"Don't force your heteronormativity on me," Rio replied with a smile. "Girlfriend. And no spawn. Never got the notion. You're a grandpa, no?"

He nodded.

"Let's get this out of the way: I, Elise Hernandez, consent to the mandatory presentation of photos."

Tom unlocked his phone. No new texts.

He joined Rio on the bed and scrolled through some of his favorites: Terra coiled in the hamper like a kitten. He and Terra after her first trip to the stylist, a luminous yellow lolly in her hand. He and Terra at Saylorville Lake. She wore a colorful knitted cap that he'd purchased for her at a roadside stand.

"She is, by any standard, adorable," said Rio as Tom returned to his chair. "Seeing anyone?"

"No," he replied. "Any time I spend in public is devoted to ducking paparazzi or scanning for anyone trying to bean me with a rock."

"I hope you're exaggerating."

"Only slightly. Your friends on the documentary are lucky I'm too dirt-poor to find a good slander attorney."

Rio leaned toward him and folded her long legs underneath her.

"I was worried you'd be grumpy. First, definitely not my friends. Don Burlington, the director? What an ass. And, second, after the screening, after I saw how they laid everyone's deaths at your feet, I wanted to pull my segments. But I'd already signed away my rights. I couldn't exactly return the money either," Rio replied.

Tom bristled a bit. "I don't blame anyone. I see the lure. Nobody left Good Weather with more than the clothes on their back. But I hope it took more than chump change for you to throw me under the bus."

Tom reached to unzip his bag. He rustled around looking for a bottle of water.

"Hey," said Rio, whistling to get Tom's attention. "It was kinda life-or-death in my case."

"How so?"

She ran a hand through her hair, revealing the rim of the wig and her bald scalp beneath. "Early stage, but it's gonna be a fight."

Tom blanched.

"I'm so sorry. I had no idea."

"Me either, until like six months ago," said Rio and laughed in a way that almost seemed genuine to Tom. "It's fine. I'm not picking out a grave plot or anything. I'll beat this. But I don't want you to think I let them string you up for a jewel-encrusted yacht or something."

As he watched, Rio attempted to resume her relaxed composure.

"Even if you had, I'd forgive you. I know you always longed to take to the high seas on a craft composed exclusively of the finest gems mortared together with caviar," said Tom.

"Her royal highness," replied Rio effecting a mock-British accent, "demands you serfs muster the S.S. Smelly Decadence at once!"

The two doubled-over in fits of laughter.

Tom wiped away a tear. "I'm glad you're here. Just Thames and I would have been tolerable. Thames, Bryce, and I would have been weird since neither of us really know him. But the four of us is a more balanced equation."

Rio whirled her hand in a flourish and gave a half bow.

"I have a rude question," said Tom.

"Oooooooo!" replied Rio. "Now we're getting to the good stuff! I'm all ears."

"Why are you here? If I were you, if Rain kicked me out, I'd have a charcoal-black taste about Good Weather. I certainly wouldn't want to sit in the same room as Thames."

"I have to make peace before the end," said Rio and clutched her hands to her chest.

She didn't get a rise out of Tom this time. Rio reached for her purse.

"Actually!" she said. She flipped through some papers and drew out a stack. "I. Want. To change your life." She enunciated each word and allowed the last few to come out in a flood. "I want to change all of our lives. Surely you didn't imagine I had no plans to right Don Burlington's wrong, did you?"

She handed the papers to Tom. He accepted the binder-clipped documents, pushed his glasses up the bridge of his nose, and began to read: "Actor release form for 'American Cult Stories.'"

"I didn't waste my time in the limelight. I went to all the parties and did my schmoozing. Don was brazen enough to invite his competition to his soirees. I liked them better. They loved me. Loved!"

Rio ticked off each sentence with ecstatic animation.

"I have a few big shots who want to start a three-part series on Good Weather. I'll be the host since I test well with audiences. Plus, I'm a survivor of *the* most notable suicide cult in U.S. history. If the three-part has good numbers, we roll on to Waco, Spahn Ranch, maybe even Clearwater Florida."

"And you want me to what? Tell my story?" replied Tom.

"Yes, that, but not just that. You are going to be my 'cult expert.' You'll have a reoccurring role. You're the sole survivor of the Good Weather community suicide. You're a figure of awe and intrigue. It'll be T.V. gold."

"Your elevator pitch is showing," said Tom. "Also, you do know that the American populace hates me, right?"

"Why do you think we want you on the show?"

He scanned over the first few paragraphs then set the contract down on the table.

"So you're gonna be the next Leah Rimini, huh?"

"Pssshhh," said Rio with a snort. "By the time I'm done, Leah Rimini's going to be begging me for an autograph. My premise is better, and the camera loves me." She jokingly posed.

Tom remained straight-faced.

"Good for you. Seriously. But I don't think it's for me. I'm still sweeping up broken glass in my own life. Throwing more stones won't help." He picked up the contract and offered it to her. Rio did not reach to accept it.

"I figured you might feel that way. But you hang onto that. This is just round one. I am going to ply you with so much alcohol and work my magic on you," she fluttered her fingers in the air, "until that most wonderful word, 'yes,' finds its way to your lips."

She perked up.

"Speaking of which…" Rio shoved her hand into her purse and withdrew a jug of vodka, shaking it lightly in the air. "Care to get us some glasses?"

Tom retrieved two cups from the bathroom. Rio uncapped the bottle and poured a healthy shot for each of them.

"You do know that it's 8:42 in the morning and that we are bound for a reunion of the most broken people on the face of planet Earth, don't you?"

"You are so right," said Rio. "We each should probably do two of these." She handed the glass to Tom.

"To the ones we miss," said Tom.

"To dreams of emerald-encrusted caviar cruisers," replied Rio.

They tossed back the glasses. The vodka was cold and immediate. Tom coughed and reached for his bottle of water.

"If you'd like to turn away, Ms. Hernandez, I'm going to change into something less slept-in before we head to our mutual gathering."

"You might recall," said Rio, reclining once again on the bed, "I have a girlfriend. Not husband or boyfriend. I'm not shopping in that aisle, hell, that whole store. You go right ahead."

Tom pulled his turtleneck over his head. He squatted and began fishing in his bag for a t-shirt.

"Shit," said Rio. "Hold up." She climbed down from the bed, her eyes fixed on Tom's scars. "I never...I mean I knew the cuts were deep, obviously. But to actually see them."

Without invitation, she ran a finger across his neck. Tom didn't want to interrupt this moment of realization for Rio, but it was embarrassing. He was vulnerable.

"Is this what you want people to see on your show, Rio? The wounds that never seem to heal?" Tom shivered as another gust of cool, sanitized air poured from a vent in the Frigidaire.

Rio looked Tom in the face, considering him for a moment. "If it will help you or someone else with injuries this deep, I'll show a thousand moments like this. Absolutely. But only if you say 'yes.' And only if it doesn't hurt you. I'm not Don Burlington."

"I know you're not," he said.

Tom pulled the shirt over his head. He turned and Rio wrapped her arms around him.

"I'm grateful to our higher power you're still alive, Tom," she said. "And no matter what happens in the next two days, release statement or no, I'm glad you're here."

Tom wanted to say he was, too, that he was glad to be here and alive. But, instead, he returned her embrace. Then he grabbed his room keys from the end table. And the two left the room, turning the light out behind them.

CHAPTER 8

From the 2020 Netflix Documentary Series *The Good Weather* "Episode 2: Shine or Rain"

(A caption reads "From the 1993 VHS Tape entitled 'Welcome to Camp Shine or Rain!' Directed by Leonard Fairbanks." The scene opens with a young woman and man in t-shirts and shorts. They jog toward the camera from different directions. Around them, blossoms tumble from the trees like tiny moths. At a volleyball court in the distance, a group of attractive youths in matching outfits cheer as one player sets the ball and another spikes.)

Man: "Well, howdy there. I hear you're new around these parts! My name is Colorado."

Woman: "And I'm Allegheny, but everyone just calls me Alle. Good to see you, C-O!"

Colorado: "You too, Alle!" (Turning to camera) "We're so delighted you want to be a part of the Good Weather community. We think you've arrived at an important moment; in fact, we think you've arrived at a turning point in human history."

Alle: "You see, our planet is facing an unprecedented

level of pollution, both spiritual and physical. World leaders are one itchy trigger finger away from incinerating every habitable continent with nuclear warheads. Television and radio producers are in a sickening race to the bottom to find the most disturbingly violent and sexual content. For-profit prophesiers arm their followers in mad grabs for earthly power while untamable disease spreads like wildfire."

Colorado: "It's a pretty sick planet out there." (Alle nods in agreement) "And while we don't believe it's the will of scripture for us to cure the whole world, we have medicine for truth seekers right here."

Alle: "But it's too beautiful a day to stand around gabbing here. What do you say we go for a walk? Maybe we can show our friends around their new home while we're at it."

Colorado: "Sounds like a cool idea to me." (He turns toward the camera and beckons.) "C'mon!"

(The film jump cuts to Alle and Colorado standing on the porch of a wooden cabin. It's clearly been recently painted and swept. The Potemkin Village quality is hard to miss.)

Colorado: "This is Superior. It's our largest men's dorm at Good Weather. If you're a fella, there's a good chance this is where you'll stow your gear and catch some zzzz's." (Colorado closes his eyes, resting his head on his steepled hands.)

Alle: (Laughs and unfolds a hand-drawn map in front of her) "But for those of us who ain't fellas, I brought this map. You should have one of these beauties in your welcome packet. They were lovingly drawn and Xeroxed by yours-truly."

Colorado: "Nice!" (He pops a thumbs-up.)

Alle: "Most of us gals bunk in Caribbean here." (She points to the map.) "Or India, right next door. There are twenty-three buildings in Shine or Rain, but don't worry; you'll only need to know a few to start. Everyone eats together in North." (She points again to the map.) "And daily services are in Estuary Chapel at the dead center of camp.

"If you're ever having trouble finding where to go next, just look for someone in a blue shirt." (Alle pinches and tugs on her tee.) "We're old hands; we'll point you in the right direction."

Colorado: "Whaddya say we pop inside and take a look?"

(The two enter the dimly illuminated dorm. Rows of bunk beds line the walls. Each bed is immaculately made. A much younger Tom Duncan in jeans and a blue t-shirt lounges on a bunk near the door. He rises to greet them.)

Tom Duncan: "Hey, honey!" (He kisses Alle on the cheek) "And hello to you too, Colorado."

Colorado: "Howdy, Ohio! I'm surprised you're not at the Atoll." (Turning toward the camera) "That's a pretty important building here at Good Weather. The Atoll is where Rain lives and where our holy scripture is transcribed. Ohio won't brag about it, but he's an important figure. He oversees the scribal transcriptions of Rain's prophecies."

Ohio: "I think everyone is pretty darn important around here." (He wraps an arm around Alle.) "But I heard you were giving a tour to our new members, and I wanted to pop by to talk about one of our three guiding principles here at Good Weather. It's called Pure Hydrology, and it's our most important.

"That name sounds kinda technical, but the principle is easy. There's so much pollution out in the world, both physical and spiritual. We don't want to bring any of that to camp. So, members of the Good Weather community refrain from partaking in any activity that is going to make us impure, that is going to pollute us. If you want to be a part of Good Weather, that means, no drinking, no smoking, no use of anything not derived from the earth, no habit-forming substances, and no gambling. And while relationships among members are absolutely a-ok, we ask that couples refrain from sexual intercourse."

Colorado: "I don't wanna be nosy, but aren't you and Alle married? Isn't that a little tough?"

Alle: (Alle snuggles up to Ohio and smiles at the camera) "Sometimes it is a little tough, C-O. But Ohio and I find other ways to show we love each other. We exchange notes. We sit in service together. And, most importantly, we spur each other on in this incredible spiritual journey we're all taking. We connect in ways that are even more intimate than sex. If we can do it, you can too."

Colorado: "Boy, I bet it feels awesome to have that kind of control, to be able to say 'My spirit decides what's right for me, not my libido.'"

Ohio: "It absolutely does. So many people who come here are under the dominion of drugs, lust, alcohol, or violent media. We offer shelter. But just like someone with a cold can carry germs, anyone who's been in the outside world can carry these sicknesses with them. Good Weather is a decontaminated zone, so we have a zero-tolerance policy when it comes to potential threats to our community."

Colorado: "Right on. Well, if you two lovebirds can make that sacrifice for the benefit of Good Weather, I bet we all can too."

Ohio: "I think you'll find you're better for it." (Ohio casts a loving look at Alle.) "But I don't want to hold up your tour."

Alle: (Letting go of her husband) "That's right! We've got places to go and people to see. C-O, how about we head to Estuary Chapel?"

Colorado: "Sounds great. Catch you later, Ohio!"

(The two wave goodbye to the cabin. The film jump cuts to a shot of the two guides in the back of an immense, carpeted chapel. Stained-glass windows, which cover the walls, cast a hazy, turquoise glow on the pews. A skylight in the butterfly roof admits an unfiltered white luminescence on the central aisle. There's no pulpit, but a small set of stairs lead to a mosaic image of kneeling petitioners peering in awe at a drizzling storm cloud.)

Colorado: (In a lowered voice) "Boy, this place knocks me out!"

Alle: "Me too! Whenever I pass through these doors, I feel the power of the true scripture. And when Rain speaks the word every night at our sundown service, *Shamayim* is just a breath away."

Colorado: "You said it. That reminds me why we're here. I'm gonna share our second guiding principle with you all. This is called Fertile Ground.

"Here in Iowa, if you want a healthy stalk of corn or a good plot of beans, you need to prep the soil. You need to clear the old, dead roots and spread nitrogen-rich fertilizer over the top. You need to build fences to keep critters out."

Alle: "And just as we need to diligently till the soil to

reap a rich crop or enjoy a beautiful garden, we need to tirelessly prepare our bodies for the teachings of the new scripture to enjoy its bounty in our lives. The contaminants of the outside world can run off into our community in all sorts of ways: through family, through old friends, through our own hang-ups. To maintain the kind of focus it takes to truly grow, members stay in the here-and-now. They commit to constant contact with their community here at Good Weather.

"Members attend a small group each morning and a late afternoon prayer intervention gathering. They finish each day with the sundown service here at Estuary. There's singing, dancing, and a telling of the holy message from our prophet Rain. Every evening is an outpouring of wisdom and truth that will touch your spirit."

Colorado: (Leaning over the back of a pew to face the camera) "Just like a good farmer doesn't want his crops to go without water for a single day, Rain doesn't want you to go without the nourishment of the true scripture here at Good Weather. That's why we ask that community members remain here at camp and forgo regular contact with outsiders. We don't allow members to own vehicles. We do have a small post office here at camp, but we use the mail service primarily for proselytizing," (Colorado holds his palm next to his mouth.) "a fancy word for spreading the true scripture.

"That might seem tough at first. But when the rich downpour starts working on you and you're humming a hymn while the sun shines down, well, all those old contaminants are gonna seem like a different life. A different you."

Alle: "If you decide you need to leave for any reason,

on your return, you'll first need to pass through our reconciliation room in Potomac Lodge. You'll go through a quarantine process that typically lasts a couple of hours, but may be longer depending on the circumstances of your departure. Any person you knew before you arrived at Good Weather, no matter how much they love you, can be a carrier for pernicious and demonic ideas. And we have to be supremely careful because enemies of the true scripture are everywhere.

"After a two-step process where you meet first with a senior member like me then with Rain, you'll be assessed. If we conclude that you've not been spiritually contaminated, you'll be welcomed back to the community and allowed to rejoin the nightly services."

Colorado: (Looking down at his watch) "Funny you should mention that. The worship crew is set to arrive any minute. We better clear out and let them get down to business.

Alle: "Roger that, C-O! How about we hit the last stop on the tour and my favorite sight here at Good Weather?"

Colorado: "Sounds like a heck of a plan to me!"

(The two walk toward the heavy wooden doors. The film jump cuts to a field where workers sow seeds. Another wave of community members in shorts and wide-brimmed hats follow after, patting the soil and singing a hymn. Their coordination is eerie, as though they were dancing to a song only they can hear.)

Colorado: "Now I don't want to sound like a cynic or anything, Alle, but why's this your favorite sight? We have no shortage of beautiful vistas, and when the orchard is in bloom...well, wow! I don't know if this compares. What's the scoop?"

Alle: "I see how you could say that. But I'm sticking to my guns on this one. And it just so happens that I have someone else here who agrees with me."

(A tall, gaunt woman with blonde hair to her shoulders steps in front of the camera. She's wearing gardening gloves and leans on a hoe. She wears a plain leather hat. She looks slightly older than either of her compatriots and the broad smile fits less neatly on her.)

Colorado: "Wow! It's Thames! If you haven't met her yet, Thames is Rain's personal attendant. Shouldn't you be getting ready for the big gathering?"

Thames: (Wiping the sweat from her brow theatrically) "Oh, I take my work shifts just like everyone else. And I love them because this is my favorite sight here at Good Weather: all of us, the greatest and the least, working together. I love getting my fingers in the soil with my friends." (Alle nods in agreement.)

Colorado: (He takes in the whole scene, tapping his finger on his chin.) "Now that you mention it, that is pretty beautiful!"

Thames: (Thames turns to face the camera.) "Our third guiding principle is called Rough Hands. We believe a hard day's work makes everyone better. This camp wouldn't be sustainable without the fruits, vegetables, and baked goods that we sell to local communities at our store. People from far and wide have heard something wholesome has its roots here at our camp. And you ought to taste our dual heaven cookies. (Thames draws a cookie from the pocket of her overalls and takes a bite.)

"The initial donation we graciously accept from new members strengthens our community's ability to spread the true scripture. But it's our daily work in the fields that keeps Good Weather growing and blooming."

Alle: "In your welcome packet, you'll find a work schedule with your shifts highlighted by yours-truly! Instructions for when and where to report are included.

"As part of the covenant agreement you signed, any revenue that you receive while in residence here should be turned over to the Good Weather community. It's a rule we all abide by. You can simply stop by the Atoll and provide the check or cash to an attendant. We'll see that it gets into the right hands. And don't worry. We'll provide you everything you need to cultivate a healthy body and spirit."

Thames: "Right on. Well, I'd love to stick around, but like C-O said, I better hustle off to Estuary and start getting ready. See you there!"

(Thames strides off-camera, and the two wave their goodbyes.)

Colorado: "We talked about a ton of important stuff today."

Alle: "We sure did."

Colorado: "We learned the Three Guiding Principles of Good Weather. Ohio told us about Pure Hydrology which protects community members from contamination by diseases of the outside world. Over at beautiful Estuary Chapel, we discussed Fertile Ground which ensures community members remain spiritually nourished. Then in the planting field, Thames taught us all about Rough Hands which keeps the community itself growing and thriving through the industry of its members."

Alle: "It may seem like a lot to remember, but if you have questions, blue shirts like me will be right there with you in the dorms, at your prayer intervention and small

KYLE MCCORD

group, on your work crew, and next to you at worship."

Colorado: "But for now, the two of us better hit the road, or we're going to be late for the sundown service. See you all soon!"

(The two give parting waves then run away from the screen in a giddy romp. The audience is left with a brief image of the sun setting on the now-abandoned field.)

CHAPTER 9

If Tom Duncan had been under any illusions about what sort of reception to expect at the Edenburg Holiday Inn, the meeting room allotted them was the nail in the coffin. He and Rio followed a series of arrows, each labeled with the ambiguous and non-threatening moniker "Camp Reunion." The arrows wended their way from the lobby into the basement of the hotel, through the janitorial supply, and past unused maintenance trollies to a door marked with a handwritten, paper sign. *At least,* considered Tom, *I know where to go if I need more soap or an extra towel.*

Rio placed her hand on the knob then peered back at Tom.

"Take a deep breath, Alice. Here comes Wonderland."

Inside, the room was comparatively pleasant. An oval table filled the carpeted conference space. Bryce and Thames had already settled in and occupied two of the office chairs scattered unevenly around the table. Bryce had, Tom guessed, arrived second and taken the seat beside Thames against her unspoken wishes. He chatted at her animatedly.

The thin blonde woman, obviously relieved by their entry, rose and approached Tom. Thames looked as though she had aged twenty years since he had seen her last. She wore a blue t-shirt and shorts. Dark bags hung beneath her eyes. She extended a stick-thin hand.

"I was sure you wouldn't come," she said.

"I was sure of that too until about twelve hours ago," he replied.

He released her grip, and a few seconds later, she followed suit. Rio had remained standing through the entirety of the exchange. She waved to catch Thames' attention. Thames stuck out her hand.

"Glad to welcome you back, Rio."

Rio laughed and patted Thames' hand.

"Awkward to see you too, hon," Rio replied.

Thames let loose a girlish giggle. It resonated off the walls of the dilapidated conference room. Bryce began to chuckle. Then Thames snorted, and they lost all decorum in a brief spell of laughter.

After they quieted, Thames took a seat and motioned for Tom and Rio to do the same.

"I'm glad you all came home. I wanted to put this weekend together from the moment that Rain and the others crested the falls. But only a few months ago did I feel a pull on my spirit telling me it was time. I invited everyone, and I wish more accepted, of course. But everyone we need is in this room. I see this as an opportunity to rebuild our faith and remember those who have already forged onward," said Thames.

Bryce raised his hand slightly. "I, for one, would like to say how much I appreciate you organizing this, Katie. I would like to present the question that I suspect everyone else is considering."

"Sure," said Thames.

"How soon can we get out of this horrific room?"

"I'm not sure we're following Robert's Rules of Order, but seconded," said Rio.

"I absolutely hear your concerns," said Thames. "I admit that the accommodations don't scream 'spiritual connectivity,' but our first chapel on Johnson in Iowa City was just a drawing room, not much bigger and certainly not better furnished than this. Remember, Ohio?"

Tom recalled the dingy, industrial workroom that had served as the first worship space for Good Weather. The space constantly smelled of sawdust and lacquer.

"As someone who also attended services in the embryonic stages of Good Weather and who recalls that space, I can testify that it was the Ritz in comparison with this place," said Rio.

"I'll organize something outside for us tomorrow," said Thames, "I was considering it anyway. The camp was sold at auction, and we can't go back. But if we hike up Pine Bluff, we'll be directly above it. That would be ideal for our remembrance service."

Bryce gave a thumbs-up, and Rio followed suit.

"I hoped we could open with a prayer: the Doxology of Water," said Thames. She reached across the table to join hands.

"It's not going to make me the belle of the ball," said Rio, breaking the silence, "but I'm going to be a definite 'no' on that. Can we pray something more universal? We're here to honor our friends who died. I know this isn't what you want to hear, Thames, but I can't divorce their passing from the reality that it was Rain's 'teaching' that led them there."

Thames placed her hands in her lap. The industrial clucking from the nearby boiler room echoed beneath the closed door. She ran a hand nervously through her stringy, yellow hair.

"I lost those friends too. And I am not here to rubber stamp all Rain's actions. But I hoped this weekend might be a chance for some of us to reinforce our faith. To rebuild what we lost. I believe The Doxology of Water is what the people who crested would want us to pray in this moment. I'd like to honor that. What did they die for if not their beliefs?"

"Our answers to that question would differ wildly," replied Rio. Tom could feel her leg frenetically tapping on the floor beside him.

"Hey, hey," said Bryce, pressing his hands down in a calming motion. "What if we prayed both? We have time."

Neither woman spoke up. Silence filled the catacomb.

"Ok," said Bryce, chewing his lip. Then he clapped his hands. "What if we have a moment of silence? And in that moment, you can pray whatever you want to whomever you want, but we'll all be focused on why we're here, which is to honor people we love who are gone."

"I don't want to be inflexible, but it's important to me to pray our community's prayer this weekend," replied Thames.

"What if we do that tomorrow at the remembrance service?" Tom said.

"Perfect," said Bryce, "I'll gladly join in then. But a moment of silent group prayer might be ideal now since we can all be a part of that."

Thames sighed, but extended her arms. The group joined hands. Water susurrated in the pipes above them. How long had it been since he last prayed? He felt like he were exercising an atrophied muscle. Tom tried to catalog the names of his friends, his friends he watched...he watched bleeding out. *What a terrible way to remember them*, thought Tom. But now, it was all that he could picture—*Colorado, his head turned sideways, and gurgling for air on the red grass.*

He felt shaky, lightheaded. Tom tried to open his eyes, but then his weight shifted sideways. He was powerless to stop it. The chair wheels skidded beneath him, and he lay on the floor. His head rang with inaudible bells.

"Oh shit," shouted Rio.

Bryce rushed toward Tom.

"No one move him. I have first responder training," said Bryce.

"Are you okay? What happened?" said Rio. She knelt next to him.

"I'm fine. I'm fine," said Tom. He attempted to sit up, but he was unsteady.

"You may be, but I'm gonna have you keep laying down for just a little bit," said Bryce. "But keep your eyes open please. Do you know if he takes any meds? Has he had anything?" He looked at Rio.

"No idea about meds," said Rio. She pulled a bottle of water from her purse and offered it to Tom. "I mean, we each had a glass of vodka in the room, but—"

"What was that?" cut in Thames. She glared at Rio without blinking. She had her phone out.

"We each had some vodka," Rio said, shifting to face her. "Oh screw you. Are you seriously going to judge me for giving my friend a drink? And who are you calling right now?"

"I'm calling the front desk to tell them that we want a medical kit down here now or I'm going to phone a lawyer with an expertise in religious discrimination law," said Thames.

"No med kit needed," said Tom, still prone. Bryce buzzed about. He took Tom's pulse and quietly and calmly asked him questions. How many fingers was he holding up? Who was the president?

From the ground, Tom continued his protestations.

"No bars," Thames said.

"Can I give him some Tylenol?" said Rio. She piled objects from her purse on the table. Thames glared at the monster vodka bottle.

"I can feel your fucking eyes on my stuff, Katie," said Rio without turning to face her. "And I'm telling you now: I don't care."

"I will add that to the laundry list of things that clearly do not concern you, Good Weather among them," said Thames, shoving her cell phone in her pocket.

Tom squirmed himself to his elbows, against Bryce's admonitions, then leaned against the wall.

"Oh that is it," said Rio, her body trembling with wrath. "I guess we're doing this now: you drag everyone back here, you pretend like nothing has changed, like the Doxology of Water isn't the mantra of a madman who killed one hundred and thirty-seven people—"

Thames attempted to interrupt, but Rio raised her voice.

"One hundred and thirty-seven of our friends! And where were you at the end exactly? I've always been a little fuzzy on that."

Thames drew back, her whole body stiff like a cat preparing to pounce.

"Why are you even here, Rio? Oh, maybe I can answer that," Thames marched close to Rio who stood to meet her. Thames pointed a lean index finger at Rio, hovering it inches from her face. "The plan goes something like this: get each of us alone, tell us your boo-hoo-sad story of poverty—oh yeah, I still have my ear to the ground—and then feed us shot after shot of that poison until we sign on the dotted line for your trashy pilot. Is that about right?"

"Go on, girl," said Rio. "What else you got?"

Bryce motioned for them to quiet down. But the keg had been lit.

Tom sagged against the wall. He felt a nausea which was unrelated to his fall. Bryce, now ignoring the verbal brawl, activated the flashlight on his phone and asked Tom to follow it with his eyes.

"Since you no longer share our faith, I figured you came here to make peace," snarled Thames. "What kind of peace are you after?"

"The kind on my own terms," replied Rio. "And I don't need your permission to find it. But I'm here to help you find some too if you'd open your eyes."

"You haven't changed one iota since Rain showed you the door. You're without the tiniest inkling of humility."

"I left, which apparently you've forgotten, and, to your second point, if it was a lack of humility that kept my throat from the blade, you'll forgive me if I don't wither at your critique."

The two women were practically standing on each other's feet. Katie loomed several inches above Rio.

Tom slid up the wall to a standing position. Bryce, apparently accepting that any further medical advice would fall on deaf ears, stationed an arm under him to steady him.

"No wonder you hate this room. There's barely enough room for even one of your agendas," said Tom. The two women turned their attention to him.

"I am here to mourn the death of my wife of thirty-plus-years who passed into the next world or maybe went over the falls with Rain or maybe just drifted into oblivion."

"Say what you need to, Ohio," said Thames, her voice now lowered. "But I can tell you for certain that she isn't gone."

"For once, you're right. She isn't dead because last night I had a lovely chat with the ghost of my dead wife. Plus, Alle is with me every day when my daughter hits a high note just a little flat while singing in the shower or my granddaughter dances when I make her French toast."

"I didn't...I didn't know you had a daughter," said Bryce.

"It doesn't matter," replied Tom. "I'm losing them both. I'm here because I can't be in their lives anymore. You'd think the bean hooks and the bodies, the scars would be the worst of it. But losing my granddaughter will finally break me. And in this dark season of my life, when I am at the absolute nadir: this scene. Well, the award for most tone-deaf emotional performance goes to both of you."

"I'm sorry about that. I am. But you don't have a monopoly on grief, Tom," said Rio. "We're coming to grips with this, too."

"You weren't there!" Tom shouted. "None of you were. I wouldn't wish that horrible moment on anyone. But don't pretend that we're going through the same thing. You didn't weather police interrogation or months of cameras. I took the rap for everyone, everyone who died, and it buried me with them. I'm just realizing how deep in the grave I am."

He got to his feet.

"I need some air."

Tom pushed his way past the door. He strode through the industrial basement following the arrows, his anger whipping him forward. Someone had turned off the light in the entryway. He felt his way up the narrow flight, but at the top, slammed his foot into the metal signpost. He yowled in pain and frustration.

He found the switch on his right then hurled the metal signpost down the stairwell. It clattered like a cymbal then came to rest. He waited to feel some satisfaction in the act. After a few moments, when it was clear none was coming, he exited into the lobby and set off in search of a bar.

CHAPTER 10

The closest bar to the Holiday Inn was the Silver Horse Pub at the Hotel Edenburg. The staff kept the lights low and the liquor, stationed in front of a series of antique mirrors, fully stocked. It was Tom's kind of place.

Every flavor of sport played on the televisions nested on the wooden beams supporting the low ceiling. A handful of scattered entourages chatted in various corners of the bar, but no one paid Tom any mind.

It had been hours since his blowup in the basement. He had expected to be drunk by now. But getting wasted before five p.m. felt like emotional labor. He'd been nursing rum and Cokes at the bar, counting his remaining cash, and watching the dazzling sunlight play on the cars in the parking lot.

On the west side of the lot, a group of skateboarding teens had positioned a board on an incline and was taking turns performing jumps. Those not on their boards watched intently, providing advice when the boarder biffed it or applauding when they pulled it off.

He finished the last of his rum and Coke. When he

lowered the glass, Alle had taken the seat beside him. She wore a blue t-shirt and brown cargo shorts.

"Uck. I love you, honey, but not that outfit."

Tom motioned to the bartender, "Can I get this topped off?"

"What can I say?" she replied. "I dress for the occasion."

Tom waited until the bartender refilled his glass and ambled toward another customer.

"I was rather enjoying sitting here, feeling sorry for myself, but I imagine you're here to ruin that."

"You used to be just like them. That's what's really getting to you."

Tom took a sip of his drink.

"I have been many kinds of awful, but if I was ever as...as self-serving as Thames and Rio, you should have cracked me over the head with a frying pan until I suffered amnesia."

"First," said Alle. "they're just scared. Both of them have way too much on the line for one weekend. Rio is afraid she's going to die without achieving any of her dreams. Thames has been hyping herself up for a reunification of Good Weather from the moment she left. Secondly, I wasn't talking about your basement buddies. I meant the boys."

Tom glanced back at the window. The boys were taking a breather from their stunts and jostled and joked in a drifting hive of teenage energy.

"I'll admit my memory has Grand Canyon-sized gaps, but I don't remember going all Tony Hawk in the parking lot of the Hotel Edenburg."

"You used to belong. We were part of something fun

and exciting that brought people together, that gave them purpose."

"Yeah," said Tom. "And it all blew up and took you with it. And when the dust cleared, I had nothing. I'm broke and reviled. And what you did at the end...I can't understand."

Alle put a hand on Tom's shoulder.

"I took me with it, not you, not anyone else." She waited a second to let this sink in. "And if that performance in the basement can teach you anything it's that our friends loved Good Weather so much that they'd drive hundreds of miles to sit in that awful room and tear each other apart. Why? Just to feel one one-thousandth of what we all experienced as a community."

"How can you say that?" Tom said. "It is all so horribly tainted by the sharpened hooks, the blood on the grass, and before that, the brainwashing, restrictions on travel, the ban on sex," Tom rolled his eyes and shook his head. "They cut us off from our own daughter, Alle!"

"You're not here to make peace with all of that. I'm not sure how anyone could in this life. But you need to remember that 'Icarus also flew.'"

Tom stared into his rum and Coke.

"You did memorize some Jack Gilbert, so at least that's plausible."

"I knew a lot more than you give me credit for. But my point is that in spite of all those horrors, these people built a world together, with you. If you're ever going to move on, and I mean actually move on, not just retreat, you need to grieve that lost world with them, no matter how fucked-up they are."

"What do you think I'm doing here?" said Tom.

"Running away. It's what you've been doing the whole time."

"I am not sure if you were absentee or something when the wanna-be paparazzi were staking out the Midwest Cult Recovery Clinic for months or I was being accosted by the justice league in the park. But when you're being chased, running is often the most rational response."

"Tom," she said and moved into his sight line. He met her gaze. With each passing day, she was becoming more a ghost, each detail of her more ethereal.

"Honey," she said, "you didn't need any prodding to find a rock to hide under. That's been the plan from the moment you were discharged from the hospital. All the rest of it has been an excuse. A good excuse, mind you. But a life built on good excuses is still just a husk of what might have been."

"I miss you so damn much."

"I know."

"I am furious at you, the real you who broke my heart."

"I know."

A commotion began in the parking lot. An attendant had finally gotten wind of the teenagers at play and in true security guard fashion was badgering them to leave the property. One boy gathered the prop boards while the others meandered back toward their van.

The afternoon sun had passed its apex and slight shadows fanned out from the nearby field. Employees for the evening shift at the casino jostled for spots in the ordered chaos of the lot.

"Hey," came a loud, slurred voice beside him. It was one of two men who'd been occupying the back booth of the bar. The speaker wore sunglasses and a dark University of Northern Iowa sweatshirt with the hood pulled up.

"Don't bug the guy," shouted his friend, still sitting in the booth.

"No, no, it's fine. I can ask him a question. I'm not looking for a blood sample or nothing," said the obviously inebriated man.

Tom finished the last of his drink and turned toward him.

"My friend Tuck and I have a bet going. Are you...are you the guy from the documentary on Hulu or whatever?"

"It's Netflix, dumbass," Tuck called after him.

"It don't matter. He knows what it's on. He was in the documentary."

The drunk man leaned his arm on the bar, feigning nonchalance.

"You're gonna lose the bet, I'm afraid. I'm not The Tiger King. But I get mistaken for him all the time. So, I see why you might think that."

The drunk friend cackled with laughter.

"Lance, leave him alone. It's not the dude anyway."

Tuck approached where Lance was making a valiant effort to remain upright.

"Oh wait, you are totally right! I owe you five bucks. This is him. Un-freaking-real!" said Tuck.

"I never agreed to be in any Netflix documentary," said Tom.

"Don't be a wise-ass," said Lance. "You may not have 'agreed to be in the documentary,'" he said, making air quotes, "but you sure as hell were in one. How come you aren't in jail? Don't murderers go to jail? Am I wrong?"

"Your friend's been overserved. It might be time to take him home before you get caught up in a drunk and disorderly," said Tom.

The bartender raised his hands and backed away from the scene.

"Let's just go back to the casino," said Tuck. "I'm feeling a hot streak coming on." He rubbed his hands together.

"I'm in no hurry," said Lance. He settled into one of the bar stools. "What'd it feel like when you offed your friends?" He ran his hand across his neck in a hyperbolic imitation of slicing a throat. "How'd you get away with that?"

"I closed your tab," said the bartender loudly. "The casino has five different bars to choose from."

Lance stumbled from his seat and knocked the stool to the floor as he did. It rattled like a dying animal. "Why does everyone seem to think we need to leave? Seems to me I've made a new friend, the Tiger King of Psychokillers."

Tom backed down from his position at the bar and removed his coat from the stool. Then, as though the rest of the world were in slow motion, a tall, dark-haired man in an overcoat shot from a nearby booth and twisted Lance's arm behind him. A woman wearing a sport coat and a cotton jumper casually followed.

"Ow, ow, oh shit, that hurts!" cried Lance.

The bartender put his hands higher in the air and backed away. Apparently, this was his signature move. Lance writhed in pain, trying fruitlessly to break the older man's grip.

"Stop struggling," said the woman, "or he's going to break your arm."

Lance went limp.

"Alright, easy choice, fellas. This is Lenny. He's a P.I., but before that he was a U.S. Marshall. He's my close, personal friend, and if I say, 'Break that dude's arm,' then whatever unlucky soul I've indicated finds himself in the hospital with a nasty case of 'shouldn't have been such an asshole-itus.'"

The woman peered at each of them as she said this, her silver eyes sharp as diamonds. She let this sink in before continuing.

"Alternatively, if I say, 'Throw that particular idiot back,' Lenny does so. Whoever he has in that death grip of his walks away with only a dent in their hubris that a few drinks somewhere else ought to remedy. Isn't that right?"

Lenny nodded, but he didn't turn his focus from Lance whose face had become a mosaic of agony.

"Now, let me ask you, what do you think I should tell Lenny?"

"Please, Miss," said Tuck, "we're happy to just walk on out."

Tuck backed toward the doors.

"My friend's an idiot. We're out of here."

"You had me at 'My friend's an idiot,' but the next sentence certainly works for me too," said the woman. "Lenny?"

He released Lance's arm. Lance bolted, keeping a wide berth of Tom.

"Bitch," he muttered. And then the two were just the whiffing of the batwing doors.

Lenny retook his seat in the booth and drank his beer mechanically. The scene had ended, and the other parties resumed their normal chatter. The woman knelt down and picked up the upset stool. She took a seat and motioned for Tom to do the same.

"Thanks."

"You're welcome," she said and settled an ornate, designer handbag in her lap. Its Klimt-esque fringes seemed to suck in all light from the bar. "How about I buy another Fat Tire and get you a refill on your," she examined the dregs in his glass, "rum and Coke?" She signaled the bartender, beckoning to each drink.

A refreshed beverage appeared before each of them. Tom was grateful, but joining her felt like entering into an unwanted compact.

"I suspect that happens to you a lot," said the woman. "A member of the average citizenry catches a glimpse of a person they've seen on T.V., and it's weird the change that overtakes them. Sort of Jekyll and Hyde."

"That sounds like an observation that grows out of experience," said Tom.

"It is. I live in New York and work for *60 Minutes*. Angela Downey."

She stuck out her hand.

"Please no," said Tom. He shut his eyes and rubbed his digits across his temples. "Look, I'm grateful, but I'm assuming this isn't a chance meeting."

"Nope," she said. She withdrew her hand and took a swig of her beer. Her eyes sparkled without offering a hint of emotion. Even without the advantage of a professional makeup crew, she was striking.

"In addition to being a pro at menacing local drunks, Lenny over there is an ace at helping me find people I'd like to talk to. I actually flew into Des Moines, but you'd already left your daughter's house for the reunion by the time I arrived."

Even buzzed, Tom felt the abrupt, sinking gravity of this disclosure. By coming to Edenburg, he may have wrecked the weekend for the other survivors. He imagined the tenuous alliance of Good Weathers climbing Pine Bluff as local reporters snapped photos from behind trees just off the trail.

Tom sighed. "You figured out why we're all here, then?"

"I wouldn't be much of a journalist if I hadn't," replied Angela.

"It's cost us so much to get to this moment. I know it's not to your monetary benefit, but I hope you might respect that," said Tom.

"Don't worry," she replied. "This is a hell of a story for someone, but it's not the story I want to tell. And I hope by keeping my mouth shut to buy enough of your goodwill that you'll take my offer seriously."

"I remain certain I'm going to turn you down flat, but I also appreciate the value of plane tickets and hired goons."

He cocked his head to see what had become of her companion. Lenny had finished his beer and was filling in a crossword puzzle.

"Hit me with it," he said.

"When the weekend is over, you come to Waterloo. I'll put you on a charter plane to New York. It'll be quiet, private, maybe even give you a chance to clear your head.

We do a primetime special, let America hear your side of what happened at Shine or Rain. Then I'll fly you home."

"You're not the first program to offer," replied Tom.

"Nope," said Angela, "But we're the best one. And I'll

give you a fair shake."

"You'll forgive the cynicism, but why should I believe that?"

"Ah," she said, "the doubting Thomas. Fortunately, I've come prepared."

Angela wiggled her arm out of the right sleeve of her sport coat. Her shoulder and forearm were a patchwork of scars and seams. They looked as though someone had written in violent, red cursive across every visible inch of skin. Tom gaped.

"In Ohio, you can get a full license at sixteen. Or, at least you used to be able to," she said. With her arm not on display, Angela took a drink of her beer. "I was driving home from a community play with my dad. It wasn't much of a play, but, fortunately, he'd anticipated that and was already half a pack of Keystones deep. He was good that way.

"He was always ragging on me for going too slowly on the open stretches, and he wanted me to take advantage of the cruise control because it saved on gas. He'd read that in *Motor Trend*. So when we got on the ramp near Fredricksburg, he started yelling about how I needed to grow some balls and trust the car to do its thing.

"About twenty minutes outside of town, it was absolutely pitch black, and something was glinting as I was coming over a hill. I hit the brake, and that woke my dad up just enough to start shouting about shitty mileage, and couldn't I just grow a pair, and why don't I listen to my old man. And while I was preoccupied with him squalling and flicking ash off his cigarette, that's when we hit the buggy."

Tom stopped mid drink.

"A piece of the dash rail flew through the windshield

and impaled my arm. I had to have five reconstructive surgeries. But that was nothing in comparison with the family who was driving the buggy."

"I am so so sorry," said Tom.

"Me too," said Angela.

She put the jacket back on.

"I became *the* story of 1988 for the Cleveland press. It was too good to pass up: 'maimed daughter goaded on by drunken dad ruins five lives at once.' Photographers followed me to school, to work, to winter formal. My date had to pick me up two streets down in a car with tinted windows.

"My dad got laid off from the steelworks, which ended up being a big win for him because it opened up hours for him to grouse to every barfly in town about his no-good daughter who hit that poor Amish family on purpose."

"Good grief," replied Tom. "Sounds like a class act."

"I've made my peace with who my dad was."

"How...how did you ever get out from under all of that?"

Angela chuckled. "I left town. Changed my name. Then I let time do its antiseptic thing."

"Do your colleagues know?"

"They're not idiots. I didn't join Witness Protection. A few Google searches is all it takes. But," she said now returning her gaze to Tom, "I'm not much of a story anymore. A day is coming when that will be true for you too. And I can help hasten its arrival."

Tom considered this woman and her unimpeachable confidence.

"Tempting. But what if, in the course of this interview—"

"Primetime special," corrected Angela.

"What if in the course of this primetime special, you determine that I'm not the Jean Valjean of my story? That I deserve some of what's coming my way."

Angela put a hand to her lips, considering this.

"You mean, what if I figure out in the course of my interrogation that you were no less culpable than Rain?"

"More or less."

"Then I'll demolish you on live television."

Tom choked on his rum and Coke As he struggled to swallow, he studied her for any indication she was kidding. He found none.

"Wow, you are a gentle soul," he remarked.

"I'm just being honest. The world needs more of that. But I don't see this whole situation playing out that way. I think you do the special, you get to tell the whole story, our viewers feel justifiably sorry for you, Don Burlington has some tough questions to answer about his fact-checking, and drunkard hillbillies stop accosting you in bars."

Tom waited for more, but Angela was done. She reached into her handbag and took out a crisp, black card. She snapped it on the bar in front of him.

"I don't believe in belaboring the pitch, so I'll just leave you with this. My cell's on there. We're here until Sunday at one. The clock on the offer runs out as soon as I'm in the air. So, you'll want to make up your mind before I leave Iowa in the rearview."

She stepped lightly off the barstool, her handbag tucked neatly in her hand. She cast a glance at Lenny, and, without exchanging a word, he stood and escorted her out of the now almost depopulated bar. Tom watched them go, then picked up the card and stuffed it in his pocket.

CHAPTER 11

It was close to nine p.m. when Tom followed the illuminated concrete pathway back to the Holiday Inn. He was embarrassed by how much of the day he'd spent contemplating Angela Downey's offer as he haunted the streets of Edenburg, periodically pausing to examine some ephemera of his old life. He liked Angela—her honesty, her brokenness hidden behind the mortared wall of her confidence. It was clear she had acted as the Montresor to her pain even if she was able to discuss it bravely.

Throughout his travels he'd intently checked his phone for text messages from Anna. There had been none.

As he sauntered toward the illuminated entrance to the hotel, two figures waited beneath the vintage awning.

"Ah ha!" shouted Rio. "We found you at last!"

Bryce stood beside her, amused by her drunken antics. Rio jogged up to Tom, examined his head, then grabbed his hand and began tugging him back toward the hotel.

"I'm sorry I wasn't here. I just needed some--"

"Nope," interrupted Rio. "We don't care about whatever you're going to say, Tom Duncan."

Rio led Tom through the lobby and past the front desk, where, mercifully, it appeared Sylvia Dennis was off duty. Bryce tailed them, obviously a little tipsy himself.

"Sergeant Bryce Benson, please bring our friend here up to speed," commanded Rio in an authoritative voice.

"Just for the record," whispered Bryce, "I was actually a corporal."

"Sergeant!" replied Rio, twiddling her finger in the air. "Don't talk back to me, or I will bust you down to corporal so fast, you'll be...you'll be most surprised by how quickly I did it."

They entered the dining room of the hotel. Neon strobes spun on a dance floor at the front of the room and couples with their children wobbled about, having fun. Beside the D.J. table, a middle-aged bride and groom held court, chatting and shaking the hands of guests.

"First, Thames and Rio made up," said Bryce. "The cage match took thirty minutes or so. I spectated. There was yelling. There was name-calling. Eventually, there was crying. They're good now. We went to the grill for dinner—"

"Too much tongue wagging, Sergeant! Get to the good part!" hissed Rio. She squeezed their procession between a banquet table of pubescent boys in dress shirts and another table where a mother struggled valiantly to keep several bibbed infants clean.

"Yes! Well, we have crashed this wedding as you may have guessed, annnnnddd..." said Bryce, "we are on a mission."

Rio launched herself into a booth on the outskirts of the room, dragging Tom along with her. Bryce scooted in beside him. It was cozy. Thames had taken the opposite bench.

"Report," said Thames, putting down a glass of ice water on a napkin.

"Phase one is complete," said Rio. "Tom Duncan is in custody."

"Does he have any idea of our intent?"

"No," said Rio.

"You should say 'negative,'" added Bryce.

"Positive, Bryce. And negative, Thames."

"That may be for the best," replied Thames, looking at Tom with theatrical sternness. "I'm not sure if this one has the mettle."

"Tom Duncan?" said Rio. "I heard he once lifted a car off an injured pedestrian. He's got the goods."

"Wait," said Bryce, breaking character, "is that true?" He drunkenly swiveled his head to examine Tom. Tom shook his head with a laugh.

"Right you are, Corporal Rio," said Thames. "I think he's ready to get in the trenches with us."

"Point of order," laughed Bryce. He set his drink down unsteadily. "I would like to note how deeply unfair it is that Rio outranks me in the fictional military when I am the only person here who served."

"We all outrank you in the faux military. But, Rio, please note that for Sergeant Bryce," replied Thames.

"Noted," said Rio and took a drink.

"Now please promptly forget it," added Thames.

"Forgotten."

"Now, since you've been MIA, Private Duncan, let me get you up to speed. In the course of interrogation this evening, Sergeant Bryce revealed an appalling wrong that is in earnest need of remedy: he does not have any recollection of Good Weather dual heaven cookies."

Tom turned toward Bryce, slapping his hands against his cheeks.

"Don't Macaulay Culkin me. I was nine when I left."

Rio lightly gripped Tom's shoulder and turned him to face the D.J.'s stand. Behind it, a door marked "Staff Only" was propped open with a dining chair.

"We have determined that the kitchen staff left for the night," said Rio, "and we intend to bake dual heaven cookies right here, right now. Thanks to Thames, we are certain the kitchen has what we need to get the job done. She has already performed renaissance on the area."

Bryce raised his hand to object but couldn't get any words out between gusts of laughter. Thames, unable to keep a straight face, joined in.

"Pull it together, troops!" impelled Rio. "In T-minus forty-five seconds, each of us is going to gather random utensils and plates from tables around the room and carry them with us to the target location. That's the cover."

"Why forty-five seconds from now?" asked Tom.

"Go!" whispered Rio. Thames shot out from her side of the table, and Tom found himself foisted out by Rio and Bryce.

Rio kept a grip on his hand. They launched toward the nearest banquet table. She hurriedly piled used plates and silverware in Tom's arms. After they'd had acquired enough props to look sufficiently servile, Rio with a few dishes in her own hand, snuck them around the increasingly bare dance floor, past the now-seated D.J., and into the kitchen where their co-conspirators waited. Tom nudged the chair into the reception, letting the galley door click shut behind him.

Forty-five minutes later, they lounged in a semi-circle on the floor of the industrial kitchen, passing around the pan of treats. Tom never understood why the citizens of Good Weather referred to these as cookies since they were more of a shortbread frosted with caramel. But he always had better things to do with his mouth when the treat arrived than argue semantics.

Rio sat with her legs extended in front of her. She had found a sliding pantry door and idly shuttled it back and forth. Bryce had located mixers and vodka in the fridge and deep freezer respectively and hovered over the prep table concocting three glasses using measuring cups and serving spoons. Thames peered into her hands. She looked serene.

"I have to be honest, Thames. I'm surprised you went along with this," said Tom.

"'Went along with this?'" called Rio, "This was her plan."

"Really?"

"What's so surprising, Ohio?" asked Thames, her head cocked in genuine curiosity.

"I mean, you were Rain's attendant. I think of you as the paragon of law and order."

"You forget so easily," said Thames, "but Good Weather was all about living your own way. At least, that's how it was for me. And, sure, the rules were pretty stiff by the end, but it started out as a band of rebels against the world."

"Why do you think I joined up?" said Rio. "I was born a rebel."

"Bryce, aren't you supposed to be the voice of reason also? The guy who shakes a stick at us and mutters something about optics," asked Tom.

Bryce walked gingerly toward the group, balancing beverages. With a practiced steadiness, Bryce handed off a drink to Tom.

"Well," Bryce said, lowering to his knees to set a glass in front of Rio. "I am concerned that Sylvia may discover us, become enraged, and move our meeting room to the ninth circle of the hotel." He paused for effect. "Oh wait!"

This got a rise out of Rio in particular, and she shot Bryce a thumbs-up.

"Are you sure you don't want a gimlet?" said Bryce.

"I'm good," replied Thames.

"But it is time to unveil the evening's entertainment!" said Rio. She drummed her hands on the floor. "You know it. You love it. It's time to play: Single Queeeerrrrry!"

"YES," replied Thames immediately, patting her hands on her knees like an eager child.

"Oh, please no," moaned Tom.

"Oh yes, Private Duncan. Surely, you didn't imagine that we were simply going to converse like normal adults. Not when we still have not engaged in my single, most favorite activity of all time from Good Weather," said Rio.

Rio shook her fists in the air in anticipation. Bryce raised his hand. Rio reached out and lowered it.

"Obviously, we never had booze when we played at Shine or Rain," said Rio, "but the way this game worked is that we would sit around the fire and each person asked someone one question, and each person answered one question. No one answers twice or asks twice until everyone has gone. No double-dipping."

"The important part of this, *the spiritual part of it*," said Thames, "is you have to answer as deeply and as honestly as possible. So, don't ask anything too pedantic or give shallow answers. Don't ask someone what their favorite color is. Think of something more meaningful."

"I need to chug some of this before what you're suggesting is possible," replied Bryce.

"Correct," said Rio. "I recommend we all do the same." She lifted her glass. "I am presenting this round as a toast to Thames: the only one of us brave enough to summon all these ghosts and lure them back to the graveyard."

"Not how I would put it," replied Thames, "but I'll take it."

Thames raised a fake glass in the air. Tom threw back the majority of the pseudo-gimlet. It hit his nearly empty stomach in an avalanche, and he coughed into his hand.

"Who wants to go first?" asked Rio. Thames, who appeared to possess some preternatural Single Query instincts, shot her hand into the air.

"My query is for Bryce," she said with a glib smile.

"Oh my," replied Rio.

"This one is sort of a softball, but it's been on my mind. You're clearly an eligible bachelor, but I see no ring. Is there a partner of some sort? Children? What's the deal?"

"Is she allowed to ask multiple questions?" asked Bryce. "I just don't want to be taken for a ride on my first time out."

"Compound questions are allowed," replied Rio.

"I feel like this is going to disappoint, but no partner, no children," Bryce replied. "My dad was a workaholic, at least according to my mother. And I inherited the gene." He shrugged.

"Not bad, newbie, but you gotta go deeper," said Tom.

"I demand satisfaction!" said Thames in feigned

outrage.

"Okay," said Bryce, mulling it over. "The last time I dated someone seriously was in college. Her name was Belinda. Very pretty, very bright. In my senior year, I got an internship in New York. I kinda hoped she'd fight for me, try to make the distance thing work, and when she didn't, well, I shut down that part of me. It was easier than you'd think."

"Doesn't your mom climb on your back about a wife and kids?" asked Thames.

"Heeeeyy," protested Rio, "no follow-up questions. Out of order."

"It's fine," said Bryce, "My mom's been fighting a losing battle against lung cancer for the past five years. She's clinging on, so I'm the tiniest blip on her radar. When we aren't talking about that, we're discussing missing money from this fund or that. My dad raided everything for Good Weather. We're still plugging the leaks. Everyone in my family has an astounding capacity for narcissism."

"That gene seems to have skipped a generation in your case," replied Thames.

Bryce smiled. Rio cleared her throat.

"Ok, since I called the game, I am absolutely taking the next turn," said Rio. "Thames, you're in the hot seat."

Thames leaned forward and rested her long arms on her knees. "I am prepared."

"Why did you leave Good Weather?"

Tom gritted his teeth as though bracing for an impact. Bryce looked down and scratched his nose.

"That's...that's maybe too much," said Tom.

"As the proctor of the game," said Thames, unfazed, "I

must remind you that no question is too personal in Single Query. And I accept the prompt, although I have to modify it."

"How so?" asked Rio.

"I did not voluntarily leave Good Weather. Rain ordered me to go."

"What?" said Tom. He felt as though he'd fallen off a ladder.

"A month before we were scheduled to pass over the falls, I decided I didn't want to die without telling Rain that I loved him not just as a prophet, but also as a man. I knew how difficult that would be. He was many, many things, but a great listener was not one of them. I cornered him in Estuary one night after service and told him the spirit that was upon me. I made him hear me," said Thames.

"I'm not sure if this is allowed, but I'd like you to detail that euphemism, 'made him hear me,'" said Rio.

"Euphemisms are allowed," replied Thames, "and a lady is allowed some discretion."

Rio shrugged and sipped more of the gimlet.

"He told me I had to leave. I asked how long, and he said until that evil departed me. I suspect he assumed I would be back in a couple days, but I'd had those feelings for him as a leader and as a man for a very long time. I planned to come back at the end, but that spark was still alive and well in me. I couldn't disobey him. So, the others left. And I'm still here because I couldn't control myself."

"That's not...that's not why you're still here," said Tom.

Thames raised her bowed head to look at him.

"Rain wasn't an idiot. He surely knew how long you'd carried that flame and that your feelings wouldn't wash away overnight. He also knew you were absolutely devoted and wouldn't disobey him. He wanted you out of the way so you wouldn't stop him."

"Then," said Thames, "it's an even colder punishment."

"If you were dead, Thames, none of us would be sitting here, drinking on the dirty floor of a hotel kitchen with long lost friends," said Rio, quietly.

Thames didn't respond.

"Ok," said Bryce interrupting the awkward silence, "I am going to give this the old college try."

"Take the reins, newbie," replied Rio.

"I have been puzzled about this since the moment you mentioned it: Tom, you have a daughter? I never met her at Shine or Rain, and everyone knew everyone."

"Anna never even saw Shine or Rain," replied Tom. "Alle and I married young. We had a small ceremony at a country church on the outskirts of West Chester. A few weeks later, we moved to Iowa City since I found a teaching job there. Our honeymoon was the trip down Interstate 80."

"I feel as though I am about to request a euphemism," said Rio.

"I will just say," said Tom, "that Anna was conceived along the way."

"I hope you at least stopped the car," said Rio.

Thames giggled.

"Anna was our little gift for five years, but the firebombing on Johnson Street spooked Alle. She didn't ever feel safe after that. I drove Anna to stay with her aunt in Davenport. It was supposed to be for a couple months, but whenever I brought up the idea of reintegrating Anna into the community, Alle said 'no.' She was worried Anna would distract her from her work. I never objected because Anna was my out. I could be all-in for Rain because somewhere out in the world I had a version of Alle and me completely divorced from Good Weather."

He could stop there. He'd offered depth. But he wanted it all out on the table.

"After I was released from the hospital, Anna came to pick me up. I think after losing her mother, she wanted me close even if I'd abandoned her. It was the first time I met my granddaughter, Terra. She has her grandmother's eyes, her unmanageable locks, and her stubbornness.

"I didn't try to leave because, honestly, I assumed I'd be in jail soon for the million crimes the cops were working to pin on me. But my public defender was surprisingly bright, and all the other witnesses were dead. So, I got off. And I just stuck around in Des Moines until two days ago when I got into a confrontation in the park after a boy pushed Terra off some swings.

"Anna says they're not safe with me there. She wants me gone for a while. She's right, of course. I suspect I might have reached the same conclusion if I wasn't so damn selfish; all I want is to spend every waking hour with Terra. But I can't put them in harm's way. So, after this weekend, I'm not sure where I go."

"Well, at least I didn't dig in a fresh wound," said Bryce. "I'm so sorry, Tom." The others around the circle echoed this.

"There's no way you could have known, but I appreciate it."

Rio had finished her gimlet and danced over to the impromptu drink station to see what remained.

"Don't scamper away," said Tom. "You're next."

Rio affected a look of coy surprise.

"I am mixing the finest elixir possible from our stolen bounty, but I am also prepared."

"Ok," said Tom, "and I hope we all bear in mind that I can ask any question, no matter how invasive."

"Booooo," shouted Thames, "get to your query."

"I was never totally clear on this: what was the impetus for you to devote yourself to Good Weather in the first place? I feel like you sort of appeared one day."

"So," said Rio. "The more direct version of your question is what am I doing hanging around with this pack of deranged lunatics, dancing dangerously close to the flames of destruction?"

"That question is more direct but twice as judgey," added Bryce.

"'Yes' to what you said and 'yes' to what Bryce said," agreed Tom.

"It was always bound to happen," said Rio, "Everyone who has ever met me knows I'm eccentric. I eat bananas sideways. As a kid, I refused to color any picture with a bird in it because I considered it bad luck.

"In 1992, I was in my second year of college, and I saw two women handing out pamphlets on campus. Some students were laughing at them, and a couple of frat guys had made a game of balling up their literature and lobbing it into a garbage can. Everyone besides the women was being a total asshole.

"I immediately decided that if all these loathsome folks hated whatever was in that pamphlet, there had to be something to it. One of those women, Tom's wife, handed one to me, and we sat on the steps of one of the academic buildings and talked for a couple hours. She listened even when I pushed her buttons, which was more than I could say for some of my professors. She was strange, sure, but she was strange like me.

"I was restless in college. I had no desire to trail blaze some new career path or become someone's paramour, and it felt like those were the only two options realistically available to me. I always thought the prescribed modes of being lacked any honest engagement with the spiritual, so when I read the pamphlet, it made sense to me.

A few weeks later, I moved out of the dorm, turned everything over to the community, and never looked back."

"Was Good Weather what you hoped it would be?" asked Bryce, totally ignoring the rules of the game.

"Yes and no. The rules were strict, and the work was hard. But community was central. People played games together; they had deep discussions about theology and significance; if you wanted to sleep under the stars, there was always someone who was game. So even if, it's hard for me to reconcile this now—"

Suddenly, there was the sound of a key rattling in the lock.

"Oh shit," said Bryce.

"I can hear you in there," came a voice from outside. Tom was struck by an immediate terror that he might again find himself before the vengeful visage of Sylvia Dennis.

"This is the wrong key," came the voice again, "and I will need to retrieve the right one from the front desk. It is my sincere hope that when I open this door, I will find the kitchen abandoned."

Footsteps sounded away from the door.

"Quickly, troops," whispered Rio. "Let us beat a hasty retreat. Discretion is the better part of valor."

They rushed toward the back exit. Rio held the door yelling "Go, go, go!" as though they were parachuting into enemy territory. Outside, the night was cool, and the old dread settled back onto Tom's shoulders like some unbreakable yoke. But he peered around at the giddy faces of his friends, and for just a second longer, released the weight long enough to feel a brief spate of joy.

CHAPTER 12

From the 2020 Netflix Documentary Series *The Good Weather* "Episode 10: F100 Tornados, the Falls at the End of the World, the Aftermath"

(A pudgy farmer in overalls sits in front of the camera. A caption identifies him as "Dwight." His face is framed with glasses which seem oversized. He rubs his huge, rough hands together. Don Burlington narrates.)

Don Burlington: "On the night of August 7th, 2019, farmer Dwight Fuller sat at his kitchen table outside Edenburg, Iowa. He was filling out forms to enter some of his more exceptional vegetables in contests at the upcoming State Fair. His wife had set kidney beans to soak for a casserole destined for a sick neighbor. Their older son had recently enrolled in classes at Iowa State University and was attending an orientation in Ames, but their younger son was upstairs completing a summer school assignment."

(The documentary switches to Dwight.)

Dwight: "About 7:30, we start hearing the siren going off at Good Weather. Because they farmed, they kept a weather siren, and whoever was in charge of it seemed to have an itchy trigger finger. So, when it started sounding, I looked over at Eda, and we both sorta shrugged.

"But after about ten minutes of it, I figured there might be something to it. I asked Eda to switch over to Channel Five, but there wasn't nothing about funnel clouds. It was weird that no one over there was tending to the siren so, I went to look out on the porch.

"There was practically no wind, and I could see the stars big and bright. Eda says I better call over there since we had a number for their store. I called, but no one picked up. That is when I started to think something was up on account of they always kept the store open kinda late."

(Dwight pinches his nose, considering what to say next.)

"Well, by this point, Keaton is come downstairs, and he wants to know why the siren is going. He can't concentrate on his math. I am at a loss because I only know but the one phone number over there. Eda thought we should call the sheriff, but it seemed like we might be overreacting. I said I'd just go over there and take a look, maybe take Keaton with me. She said there was no way in hell he was going near that camp.

"So, I set off by my lonesome. I start coming through the west pasture, and I see they got a bonfire going out on the soccer field. Like mammoth logs stacked skyward. So, as soon as I seen that, I took out my cell to dial the sheriff because one loose bit of kindling, and you got a prairie fire for sure. The sheriff, Sam, and I went to high school together. He knows I don't call unless it's something serious. The call rings right through to him. I told him about the siren and such. He said he'd get a deputy and come down.

"When I get off the phone with him, I figure I'll go see if someone is at least tending that big fire. There's a slight rise when you hit the windbreak. So, when I got there, I spied over the wire gate because from there you could see down the slope and onto their soccer field. Once I got a good look from there, I stopped dead. (Dwight shakes his head.) I couldn't believe it."

(The interview cuts away, and the screen fades to black. The final chorus of "American Pie" by Don McClean plays. Then the documentary shows the image of a tranquil creek passing through woods. On the bank opposite the camera, a doe laps at the stream.)

Burlington: "It all began with water. In 1992, Leonard Fairbanks used the earth's water cycle as the central metaphor of Good Weather, as the lynchpin of his argument for a whole way of life. In a decade when Iowans were ever more aware of their tenuous relationship with that precious resource, the message rang true. Good Weather grew dramatically, and Rain positioned himself as the messianic figure of his own faith."

(The doe catches sight of the camera crew and recesses into the woods.)

"Sadly, water was also the Good Weather community's undoing."

(The documentary cuts to found night vision footage of a storage closet in the Atoll compound. A hand pulls open a closet door. Inside are pharmaceutical bottles stripped of any identifying marks.)

"According to forensic toxicologists and detectives who examined the property, it appears that in early July of 2019, Leonard Fairbanks began spiking the Good Weather community's water supply with a cocktail of crushed morning glory seeds, salvia, and psilocybin. The latter he was able to obtain with the help of a pharmacologist named Lindsey Stenson who was an on-again, off-again member of Good Weather since the early 2000's. Officers believe Fairbanks blackmailed Stenson, who later killed herself.

"Toxicology reports revealed Fairbanks did not drink the tainted water himself. But even without ingesting drugs, by July, he had become increasingly erratic. In his sermons, he focused on an event alternately called F100 or 'cresting the falls at the end of the world.'"

(The documentary cuts to a recording of Rain as he speaks in Estuary Chapel. Sweat beads his bald head. He wears long robes which trail behind him. He prowls back and forth on the stage like a panther stalking the edges of its cage.)

Rain: "The world out there, it's just getting sicker and sicker, y'all. Sicker and sicker. When we started Good Weather, we were worried about what? Plastic in our waterways, shoot 'em ups on evening television, promiscuity on campus, divorce, increasing CO^2, and spiritual decay and deadness in our churches. And don't get me wrong, all of that, whew, it was overwhelming. The world needed and still needs the Good Weather message. Am I right?" (He points to the audience who clap in agreement.)

"But the kinds of sickness now, man, it's hard to even take the pulse of it all. Pornography at the touch of a button, on demand, any hour of the day, polar ice caps melting, whole states on fire, phony, for-profit pastors living in their mansions..." (Several community members boo.) "Yeah, shame on them. They're gonna be begging for the good rain to fall when they're burning in the great flame. But they're gonna be chained to those flames, not a soul in the world to save them."

(Rain races forward in a sudden, manic motion and raises his voice.)

"True scripture, pour down upon us! Oh true scripture, make us the good well!" (Members of the community howl in agreement, some speaking unintelligible prayers.)

"But I had another message last night. And this is important, so listen up." (A hush comes over Estuary) "I was sleeping in my bed up at the Atoll. Suddenly, I hear this voice calling me, and I'm awake." (Rain snaps his finger.) "In front of me, there's this angel. But he's different than any angel I've seen before. His body is the complete absence of light, pure darkness, and there's wind swirling inside him. It's furious and howling like he's made of weather itself. When the angel speaks, its voice is pure thunder.

"At first, I'm paralyzed. But then it says 'Arise, Rain the Prophet, for I have a message for you from the true scripture.' So, I shoot out of bed and grab a pen and pad off the nightstand, but the angel says, 'The message I bring must be inscribed in flesh.' He reaches out and lays a single finger of pure darkness on my temple."

(Rain mimes the motion, gently reaching to touch an audience member. Rain is unctuous with perspiration and pants heavily.)

"And I feel this insane burning like someone is drilling through my skull. I thought my brain would explode. But when he's done: I *know* what I'm about to tell you now as though I'd written it a thousand times. I *know* it like I know the sound of my own voice.

"Here's the news: the big finish is coming. The end of the rat race. The terminus. The falls at the end of the world are just ahead. We're going over first because you won't like what comes next if you stay. You won't. Our place in *Shamayim* is ready, so we need to GTFO: get the 'eff' out, my friends."

(The crowd is silent. Then the front row rise and applaud and others follow. 'Where's the boat, and when do we leave, Skipper?' calls a voice from off-screen.)

"Well, Volga, you're already on the boat, ya wackadoo!"

(Laughter)

"It's right here. This temple. But when do we leave? Now that is tricky. I might need your help with that one. After he seared the true scripture into my memory, the angel led me to my window. And listen close, y'all. The soccer field was a giant coastline. Spires of rock and thousand foot crashing waves. There was a big serpent throwing fish into its open mouth, and I could tell that was the malevolence, our enemy, the one polluting our world, as we speak.

"And as I'm watching, the mist moves off the shore, and I beheld a golden boat with masts as tall as this roof, maybe twice as tall and pure silken sheets falling down from every one of the yards. It was unbelievable, y'all. My breath caught in my throat, and the angel said, 'Any who join you in the craft will be saved, but all who remain behind shall be swallowed by the serpent.'

"He pointed at the serpent, and it let out a terrible yowl so that my bones rattled in my body. And I felt my *nephesh* dance in my throat."

(Rain genuflects to the floor.)

"I fell down praising because so many of you will be

saved, and I begged that none be left behind. Then the angel lifted me up and told me that we must watch for the appointed time. I asked when we should set sail, and the angel said this:

'Many will have dreams and visions, and that will be your only sign.'

"Then, the angel drew a golden sword. I was afraid so I bowed my head. But he dove headfirst into the winds, into himself. And he was gone. When I looked outside, the beach and serpent had vanished, but I heard that shattering yowl. I believe it was a warning to anyone who doubts the moment is coming."

(Rain pauses, visibly shaking, and sits on the step. He looks sallow and emaciated. He motions for someone off screen to bring him a drink. Thames rushes toward him with a bottle of water and a towel. He accepts both, and she retreats off screen.)

"Now who..." (Rain pauses to chug part of the bottle then place the towel on his head) "who here has been having dreams? Maybe seeing visions?"

(Hands shoot up all over the chapel. Soon, every hand in the building is raised.)

The documentary cuts to a man in a grey dress shirt and slacks, who a caption identifies as "Agent Ed Sampson, FBI Psychologist." The wrinkles landscaping his countenance are indicative a man who worries for a living.)

Agent Sampson: "You can see from the tapes that Fairbanks had lost touch with reality. In June, Fairbanks passed out and was taken to a hospital where doctors discovered he had pancreatic cancer. He recovered there for a few days. Community members were told that he was at a summit of world religious leaders. It looks like Lisa

Duncan hushed up any rumors about his diagnosis.

(The documentary displays hospitalization records from Waterloo Lutheran General then cuts to an image of Rain with his head bandaged, his face badly swollen.)

"We believe he wanted his followers to die with him. What anyone with the most modest psychological training sees here is a psychopathic narcissist. And this guy, he had a lot of power. That got a lot of people killed."

(The documentary cuts to the image of a large brick shop on a promenade. The promenade faces out on the raging Mississippi. Cars bustle back and forth in front of it.)

Burlington: "In late June, Good Weather Ministries placed a rush order for one hundred and thirty seven bean hooks from Bud's Agricultural Supplies in Burlington, Iowa."

(The documentary cuts to a stocky man. He and his son sit behind a sanded wood counter built out of the trunk of a thick tree.)

Bud: "No, it wasn't unusual to get orders like this, especially during the summer."

Bud's Son: "Yeah, people set up business, or have an abundant harvest. They need a ton of hooks."

Bud: (Spitting chew into a cup) "It was late in the season, I admit. That was odd."

Bud's Son: "For sure. But we figured maybe the whole church was helping a local farmer. Not our business to ask."

Bud: (Nods in agreement, his bulging arms crossed in front of him.)

(A series of black and white images of bean hooks with police tags plays across the screen.)

Burlington: "The order arrived in early July. The bean hooks were distributed to families. Adults were supplied tools to sharpen the blades.

"On the afternoon of August 7th, members of the Good Weather community came in shifts to the camp woodshop. Any bean hooks which weren't razor-sharp were immediately 'fixed' by the woodworkers.

"At 5:30, all community members reported to North Lodge."

(The documentary returns to Tom's police interview).

Dodson: "Walk me through the events of August 7th after you arrived at North Lodge."

Ohio: "Alle and I arrived around 5:15 p.m. She'd been sick most of the day with a fever and vomiting. When we arrived at North, I hunted for a garbage can in case she needed to throw up, but other members of the community had already taken them. Eventually, we pulled in next to another family who brought their own."

Dodson: "Did you find it odd that so many people were all ill at the same time?"

Ohio: "At Good Weather, when one person got sick, everyone did. But Rain also told us that a pandemic of unparalleled proportions would sweep the globe. We figured it had arrived. We were trying to keep our loved ones alive until the ceremony."

Dodson: "What did you believe would happen if you didn't die in the ceremony?"

Ohio: "We believed anyone who didn't board the ship was food for the malevolence."

Dodson: "Your version of Satan?"

Ohio: "They're not equivalent, but if that helps you understand it, sure."

Dodson: "Do you believe that now, that you're simply food for this malevolence?"

Ohio: "Does it matter?"

Dodson: "Not really. I'm mostly curious. What happened after you and Alle joined the other family?"

Ohio: "One of the attendants said a blessing—"

Dodson: "Where was Rain?"

Ohio: "As we learned later, Rain was preparing a bonfire. The North staff had cooked beef stew, and Alle thought it might help to settle her stomach if she ate."

Dodson: "Did you suspect at the time that the food was laced with ecstasy?"

Ohio: "No."

(The documentary cuts to a map of Shine or Rain. North Lodge, the soccer field, and the camp weather tower are all marked with X's. Lines cross the map as Burlington narrates.)

Burlington: "After their meal, community members were led to the soccer field by a group of attendants. Some parents carried children. Families assisted elderly relatives.

"A giant bonfire was lit and crackling. Rain, flanked by attendants, offered a prayer of invocation by megaphone. He led the community in reciting the Doxology of Water, a community prayer."

(The documentary cuts back to the police interview.)

Dodson: "I need you to tell me what happened next. It is going to help a lot of families understand if they hear it from you. You said that's why you wanted to talk, right?"

Ohio: (Takes a drink of water, his hand visibly shaking) "After the invocation, Rain approached each family to offer them a blessing on their journey to *Shamayim*. Just a few words. He would run a finger down each person's nose. His fingers were covered with ash. Then...then whoever was oldest slit the throat of one family member after another. A few small children tried to run, but the attendants caught them and finished the job. Then the parent cut their own throat. Or there were attendants if they couldn't.

"Once all of them were dead, Rain passed on to the next family.

"Alle...Alle didn't want to put that on anyone else. She said we had to do it ourselves. She said she wanted it to be me.

"Rain finished with the family before us, the ones who shared their garbage can. Rain looked us both in the eye, he put a hand on Alle's shoulder, whispered in her ear, then...Alle slit my throat before I even got my bean hook out. There was still so much blood. I passed out and fell forward. Everyone assumed I died."

Dodson: "But you did not slit Lisa's throat? I just need you to confirm that."

Ohio: "No. We, Alle and I, we wanted to go together. I still don't know why she did what she did."

(The documentary fades to black then cuts to a nighttime image of the soccer field. A sober folk melody plays. The field itself is silent but for the noise of cicadas. The sporadic flash of lightning bugs breaks the darkness. The fallow field looks like a scene from Chernobyl with all its waste and poison.

The documentary switches the shot to an FBI agent seated in a lab. The germless, achromatic room stands in stark contrast to the dark field just shown. A caption identifies her as "Alicia Waters, forensic crime scene reconstructionist.")

Agent Waters: "Here's what we know about the last hour or so of Leonard Fairbanks' life. You will see that it is inextricably intertwined with Lisa Duncan's. Some of this is informed speculation, but most of it is undeniable from the forensic evidence.

"Fairbanks attended and participated in the mass suicide and, in some cases, mass murder. One attendant was Lisa Duncan—she had not only her husband's blood on her, but the blood of thirteen other people.

"When most of the killing was over, there were eight people left: Fairbanks, Lisa Duncan, the five other attendants, and Tom Duncan—who, inexplicably, had not been checked for signs of life. The other five attendants gathered in front of Fairbanks and Lisa Duncan. She slit their throats while Fairbanks watched. We know this because she had blood from each of them on her, while Rain had none.

(Waters pauses to rub her head.)

"Now here's where it gets even creepier, if that were possible. After killing the other five attendants, Fairbanks and Lisa Duncan moved to a nearby blanket close to the wind siren and engaged in sexual intercourse. There is trace evidence of this on the blanket, together with Fairbanks' robe and Lisa Duncan's clothing discarded there. Mind you, this was while Lisa Duncan was covered in the blood of numerous victims.

"After that, either Fairbanks or Duncan activated the wind siren, knowing that it would take many minutes for anyone to arrive at the scene. Then the two of them walked naked to a nearby garage where a Chevy Suburban was parked. They put a garden hose into the tailpipe then threaded it through the vehicle's slightly open rear driver's side window. Maybe they had prepped this in advance; we simply can't be sure. Then they climbed into the backseat, intertwined, and succumbed to carbon monoxide poisoning before the police arrived. They experienced a far less traumatic death than the other members of the cult."

(The documentary returns to Dwight.)

Dwight: "When I got back to the house, Eda and Keaton seen I was spooked. They wanted to know what was out there. I told Keaton to go to his room, but Eda started crying and said she wanted him right here with us.

"I called the sheriff and got the dispatch. I told them to call Sam, tell him something terrible happened down at the camp. I seen all kinds of bodies, and I don't know if it were murder or what.

"All the while, Eda's tugging at me, asking what I seen. But then she heard that last bit about murder, and she fetched the rifle from the basement closet and got the bullets out of the top cabinet.

"When I got off the phone, Keaton, he wanted to know about Miles, one of the boys from down at camp, because they used to play ball together before the cult forbade it. He kept asking was Miles alright? Was he one of them I seen?" (Dwight removes his glasses to wipe a tear from his eye.)

Interviewer: "What did you tell him?"

Dwight: "I said I didn't think no one down there was alright."

(The documentary cuts to an image of police lights.)

Burlington: "Sheriff Sam Mills and Deputy Lena Wan were the first to arrive at the scene."

(The documentary flips to a young Asian woman in her police uniform who a caption identifies as "Deputy Lena

Wan.")

Deputy Wan: "While we were inbound, we received an update from dispatch that we were potentially dealing with multiple homicides. Based on that, we determined it was better to approach the camp rec field from the highway. If there were survivors, we wanted to render them assistance as soon as possible, but we had no idea of the situation on the ground.

"Sheriff Mills positioned the car along the shoulder. He indicated to me that he intended to approach on foot while I covered him from the vehicle. At that time, the wind siren continued to sound, which made communication difficult.

"After three to four minutes, Sheriff Mills returned and told me there were at least ten bodies on the field. He ordered me to contact dispatch and have them send EMS services from Edenburg and North Castle. He said that once I'd done so, I should help him provide medical assistance to anyone still alive.

"At that time, neither of us had any sense of the scope of the massacre. We were concerned it might be some sort of mass shooter event.

"When I approached the scene, I first encountered a middle-aged man and two girls, roughly ages five and eight. It appears the girls had tried to flee. Their throats had been violently cut. The two girls lay face down, heaped on one another, but the man was face-up. He had a bean hook in his hand, which I presumed to be the murder weapon. I was examining each of the bodies for a pulse when Sheriff Mills approached me. He looked very ill.

"He warned me what I should expect when I approached the rear of the bonfire. I had never seen Sam, the Sheriff, so worked up. He said that he believed that everyone on the soccer field was already deceased.

"Sheriff Mills ordered me to find the control box at the base of the weather tower and disable the siren. I left to do so, and Sheriff Mills continued rescue operations for any survivors." (She pauses.)

"I realize now that his intent in ordering me as he did was to keep me from what was on that field." (She thinks to herself.) "I am grateful to him for that."

(A subtitle at the bottom of the screen reads "Sheriff Mills declined interview." The documentary cuts to an EMT who a caption identifies as "Alisha Chester, Edenburg EMT Services.")

Alisha: "Ralph Dennis and I were close when we got the call, just a few miles out. We passed the gates then took a gravel path by North Lodge. At that point, Ralph spotted Sam. Sam flagged us toward the soccer field. When we were about forty yards out, he held out a hand for us to stop.

"We got out of the ambulance, and I immediately realized why he cut us off short. Ahead were a family of seven to eight people all just prone in the dirt. One of them, an elderly man, his shirt was black with blood. None of them were moving.

"Ralph, he was greener than me. I don't think he'd ever been to a murder scene before, but he tried to rush over to the bodies before Sam stopped him.

"Sam said, 'You can't help them. That right there is done.'

"Sam called me over since it looked like Ralph might need a second. He said that Lena Wan was on site too. He informed me that he'd already swept most of the field. About that time, we started to hear a low moaning from close to the bonfire. One of the people near the firelight began moving. Sam drew his firearm and the two of us walked carefully toward the sound.

"Tom Duncan managed to roll over, and I realized immediately that his throat was badly lacerated. I set to work stabilizing and bandaging him to reduce the danger of sepsis. He was in shock and badly dehydrated."

(The documentary shows grisly photographs of the scene of the suicide. In the background of each, the titanic bonfire rages like an unappeasable beast.)

Burlington: "The EMTs rushed Tom Duncan to Lutheran General in Waterloo where he received a blood transfusion and was taken to surgery. Duncan remained in the intensive care unit for three days before his condition stabilized.

"Blood toxicology reports found that Duncan had four psychotropic substances in his system, three at dangerously high levels. Tom Duncan is the sole survivor of and witness to the Good Weather suicide."

(The documentary cuts back to Tom's police interview.)

Dodson: "So much of this baffles me...I just can't get in your frame of mind, but what puzzles me most is this: why did you and Rain decide that you, Tom Duncan, should be the sole survivor? What's the plan from here?"

Lawyer: "Annnnnnnd, we're done. My client agreed to this interview in spite of my legal counsel. He is not here to answer bad faith questions."

Dodson: "Maybe I've been asking the wrong questions. How did you trick Alle into thinking she killed you?"

Ohio: "Sounds like you have a theory. Everyone who wasn't there seems to have one."

(The lawyer glares at Ohio, but Ohio waves him off.)

Dodson: "Did you help drug everyone to get revenge on the community that had stolen your wife from you, that turned a blind eye on Rain fucking your wife?"

Ohio: "That is your theory? I'd say you're grasping at straws, but that would be too generous."

Dodson: "I mean, it had to drive you crazy. What kind of man would knowingly let his wife do that with someone else? Alle would do anything for Rain. She was in love with him."

(Tom begins shaking his head. Tom and his lawyer rise from their chairs and head for the door.)

Dodson: (Standing and following Tom as he exits) "Rain's gone, Tom, and he took your wife with him. But you're still slinging his bullshit. That's gotta be nearly impossible to live with!"

(The documentary fades to black then cuts back to footage of a prosecutor behind a podium. The sounds of press can be heard. A caption reads "News conference in Eden Country one month after the killings." Cameras click and flash.)

Reporter: "Is Tom Duncan going to be charged with anything?"

Prosecutor: "As of now, he is not going to be charged with a crime."

Reporter: "Can you explain?"

Prosecutor: "The evidence does not support charges at this time, but we are holding our options pending any new evidence."

Reporter: "Didn't Duncan know about the planned suicide and do nothing?"

Prosecutor: "I worried this might generate some confusion, so we've brought in an expert. This is Professor

Lon Griffith, a criminal law expert from Drake University. He has been consulting with us on this case."

(A man with small glasses and a great grey beard approaches the microphones.)

Professor Griffith: "What the prosecutor is saying, without actually saying it, is that Tom Duncan is almost certainly *never* going to be charged. Here's why: the crime scene reconstruction paints a clear picture of what happened. Tom had only his blood on him. For Tom to be charged as an accomplice in any of the other killings would require that he have committed some act to aid the other killings, with the intent to do so. While such evidence may exist, it is only within the mind of Tom Duncan—and he's not talking.

"So, there simply is no available evidence that he committed an act to aid the other killings, or intended that they occur. Sure, he knew the other killings were going to happen, but in the eyes of the law, knowing something is going to happen, without intending for it to happen, is not sufficient for accomplice liability.

"The prosecutor and I have discussed whether Tom could be charged for conspiracy to commit murder. But that would require proof that he had entered an agreement with some other person or persons that these killings would be committed. Again, there is no evidence of that, other than possibly within Tom's mind.

"Thus, as hard as it may be to swallow, Tom's sole legal status is as a victim of an attempted murder committed by his wife.

"Of course, many people are seeking to affix blame to Tom Duncan because they are appalled by the beliefs he held as a member of this cult and by his willingness to participate in the mass suicide. However, a person's beliefs and associations are protected by the First Amendment and accordingly are not criminalized under the Iowa Code. While attempted suicide is a crime in some states, it is not in Iowa. So, from a legal standpoint, he cannot be proven to be a criminal even if, from a moral standpoint, what we suspect he did is, well, monstrous. There's no other way to put it."

(As Professor Griffith steps down from the podium, reporters shout further questions into the void. The documentary fades to black.)

PART 2

CHAPTER 13

Tom had been awake for roughly an hour when, at 6:07 a.m., someone knocked on his hotel room door.

He'd showered then taken a seat by the window, resting his legs on the ottoman. Out the window, a slow trickle of wedding guests packed their vans and SUVs, some carrying still-sleeping children on their shoulders. They shimmied overnight bags under seats, settled snacks in cup holders, and performed intricate games of Tetris with trunk space.

What separated them from him besides this sliding glass window? The answer was simple: they had more ahead of them than behind them. Over the horizon lay home, whether trailer or mansion.

Last night he belonged, if only for a moment. When the survivors parted ways after the kitchen raid, he basked in that moment of connection. He'd waited so long to settle back into the herd, and for an hour, it seemed possible. But he was conscious, even in the moment, that it was a temporary reprieve. Now, that feeling flitted away like the wedding guests, and the sun rising on a new day offered no guarantees.

Tom's left foot had fallen asleep. When he heard the knock, he hobbled to the door, the flame of circulation reigniting his nerve endings. Outside, Thames waited, dressed in a blue and orange jogging suit, her blonde hair pulled back in a bun.

"C'mon," she said, "we'll hit the continental breakfast and roll."

"Could I haggle you down to treadmills in the workout center?"

"Workout centers are for corporate slugs with no connection to the natural world," replied Thames.

"I have to check my available attire," said Tom, glancing at his clothes splayed out on the room's unused bed, "but I doubt I brought anything close to workout gear."

"What you have on is fine," said Thames, motioning him to follow. "We'll powerwalk."

She led them down the highway for roughly a mile before they swerved onto a hiking trail. The length of her strides exceeded Tom's though he nearly matched her prodigious height. He struggled to keep up without jogging. Eventually, she recognized his difficultly and slowed her pace to match his.

"I hope I didn't interrupt your meditation. Have you decided where you'll go next?"

"What makes you so certain that was on my mind?" replied Tom.

"My calling for thirty years was attending to another person's needs. I learned to anticipate what Rain thought and felt. Hard to turn that kind of intuition off."

Globular red berries dropped from an overhanging tree, joining others that formed a crimson mush on the asphalt. Thames made no effort to sidestep and squished one as they continued.

"It's weird," said Tom, speaking slowly. "You spend so long adapting to one particular person, building a telescope to peer into the tiny kingdom of their thoughts and feelings. And when they're gone, all you can do is reverse that instrument back on yourself. But, at least for me, the last thing I want to do is see through that aperture."

Two morning joggers clopped by, hailing them as they passed.

"That's why you didn't answer my question, right? You don't want anyone else to use that telescope either?"

It was too early for this kind of directness.

"You ever wonder," he replied, "if your combination of incisiveness and honesty is a gift or a curse?"

Thames lowered her eyes. Tom weathered a flush of cold, as though a ghost had passed through him and floated further along the path ahead.

"I suspect that was a dig, but I've considered it often," she said.

"I'm sorry," replied Tom. "Sometimes in the morning... I get caught up in myself, and my mouth gets ahead of my brain."

"I don't expect to dollop out honesty," replied Thames, "and have it spoon-fed back to me."

Still she increased her pace, signaling her displeasure.

They passed several minutes in silence. The storage facilities and warehouses on the outskirts of Edenburg gave way to open country: a wide field of marigolds humming with insects, a canopy of branches crisscrossing the pink sky over the path. A long light vaulted out of the western horizon. Perhaps the others were rousing for the day.

"I am a fearful that I already know the answer, but does this morning constitutional have a destination?" asked Tom.

"I thought the two of us, those who still have faith, should see Shine or Rain first. We need to face what happened, just the two of us."

Tom came to an abrupt halt. Thames continued a few more paces then realized that he was no longer beside her. When she turned, Tom hunched low to the ground. He sat, hugging his knees. His heart felt like a gong slammed over and over.

Thames crouched next to him, inspecting him with a forensic interest.

"You can't ask me to go back. Alle died there. I watched dozens of our friends bleed out."

"Alle and dozens of our friends crested the falls at the end of the world there," corrected Thames.

"Honestly, I don't get it: how can you still believe any of Rain's teachings? After all you've heard since he died? He was drugging the water!"

Thames rolled back off her heels. She closed her eyes and pressed two fingers to her right temple.

"Rain made mistakes, but that doesn't mean our faith is meaningless. And do you really believe that hit job documentary? Tom, they dressed you up to be a conspiratorial murderer." She jabbed a finger in his direction. "Don Burlington and his team of professional liars are the reason you don't have a home."

"The reason I don't have a home is because I kept my mouth shut first about the travel restrictions then the 'reconciliation room.' I drank the Kool-Aid because I didn't want to rock the boat. I didn't want to believe that a man I devoted decades of my life to, who I considered a prophet, was a deranged lunatic. Hell, I'm still compelled to believe his bullshit on my bad days."

"Running a community means constructing rules and setting boundaries. And Rain *was* a prophet, even if he was deeply flawed," replied Thames.

Thames' jawline was stiff, and her blue eyes flashed with conviction. She looked cornered and vulnerable.

Joggers passed heading the opposite direction. They moved stealthily, trying to avoid entanglement with the two figures seated on the ground.

Thames pushed off the asphalt and offered Tom a hand.

"I'm happy to continue this conversation en-route to the camp. But we are blocking the pathway."

Tom did not reach for her hand.

"I'm not going back."

"Well," said Thames, considering. "By my estimation, you're too polite to sit there and impede others. So, it's either forward or backward. Now consider that if I am wrong and everything we believed at Good Weather was a lie, you still need to face your demons. So, there is only one way here, fella."

Tom desperately wanted to scourge her smug certitude, to pierce her with a sharp retort. But he'd already tasted blood in their conversation, and it hadn't been to his liking.

He bypassed her hand but picked himself up and

walked at a slow gait in the direction of the camp.

The entrance to Camp Shine or Rain was inaccessible by foot. The county put up barriers, including an immense chain link fence, to keep out the curious. And overgrowth served as an effective deterrent for all but the most determined wayfarers. But the soccer field and now dilapidated Estuary Chapel remained visible from the highway.

Tom completed the last leg of their journey in silence, instead taking in the dramatic changes. He marveled at how, with no one to restrain it, nature had reclaimed the camp. Dense foliage climbed the remains of the dorms. The once-even rows of corn were gone, replaced with huge patches of crabgrass. When they reached the overlook, Thames remained standing. Below, no traffic moved along the remote highway.

The soccer field was barely discernible but for the lack of trees. No matter how irrational, Tom expected blood to stain the weed-choked plateau. He expected the trees to have marched away from this place of mass death. *Great Biram wood to high Dunsinane hill shall come against him,* he thought. He narrowed his gaze, trying to catch some outline of the pit where the enormous bonfire had raged. But there was nothing.

"It's all...it's all gone," he said.

Thames peered over at him solemnly, nodding. He recognized immediately that she misunderstood his meaning.

"You said yesterday that you weren't sure where Alle is now," said Thames. "Honestly, that makes me sadder than our desolate chapel or our ruined camp."

"I want to believe that Alle, that all of them, are in

Shamayim. I do. I know you loved her just like I did. But how can I feel that way anymore? Rain became...he became an anaconda choking the life out of Good Weather. And his grip got so strong until there was no air left for anyone."

"You used to have some faith. You used to really believe," replied Thames.

Tom tried to cut in.

"Even if Rain was sick, like you say, do you believe the true scripture couldn't speak through him? Couldn't use him? Surely, you didn't believe he was a perfect conduit when you met him. I loved him, but I wasn't blind. I always knew he had flaws like any other man. But Good Weather was more than just Rain. It was the true scripture, the community."

"But he ruled over us by the end," said Tom with a sigh. "He was a hypocrite. Do you have any idea how much of Atlantic's money he burned through?"

"He lived a monastic life. No one knows that better than me."

"Oh, come on, Thames!" He leaned his head back in exasperation. "Are you really still toeing the company line on this? I worked in the Atoll. I saw the expense reports. By the end, I stayed in spite of Rain, not because of him. The most luxurious monks in the world didn't live like he did."

Thames remained close-lipped. This time she didn't push back.

"Don't...don't you believe we'll be together again? With all of them?" asked Thames. For a moment, her voice was plaintive and girlish.

"I'm not sure. Maybe not in the way we believed. But I

hope so," said Tom.

"I wish you had more than just hope left," said Thames wistfully. "When everyone was gone, I imagined you were still out there somewhere, believing just like I did. Because if it's just me, if I'm the last one left..."

"Thames—" began Tom, but Thames cut him short.

"I have this dream where I'm down on the field," she pointed. Tom noticed tears pooling at the edge of her averted eyes. "It's dark outside. It's one of those winters when the stars seem so far away, and the moon is a cold, lifeless orb. I can see my breath. I keep calling out to see if anyone is out there, but I don't hear anyone. I reach in my pocket, and I can feel a lighter there. It's this metallic Bic that I won at a carnival when I was a kid.

"I raise it in the air, and in the distance, I can see someone is doing the same. I start walking towards them, slowly, because I don't want to trip over all the exposed roots and vines. But they're headed the other way. Calling just like me. I hold the light higher, but they go around the corner of a building. I yell and yell. I'm sure that if I can get to whoever it is, we can cross over. We can pass out of the dark field and go home."

Tom waited for her to finish. A U-Haul thundered down the highway, the sound of its motor filling the whole valley. Then the cacophony faded. He realized suddenly that she was done.

"Do you ever reach the other light?" he asked.

"Not in the dream, but I hoped to here."

After a few seconds and without any further exchange, Thames set off toward the hotel. Whatever she'd come out here to find, she was no closer. And he had wounded her. That was apparent to Tom.

He gave a second glance to the field where his wife slit his throat. He allowed himself to feel the unbelievable hurt of this. For an instant, he longed to hold his pain close to him, to swaddle it like a child. Then he let this go and retook the road.

CHAPTER 14

At one that afternoon, the Good Weather members assembled in the parking lot where the day before Tom watched the skateboarding boys being escorted off hotel property. Bryce appeared to have packed for the occasion, sporting a Benson Seed Supply cap, shorts, and a ribbed tank; Thames had changed into a breezier outfit than she had worn for the morning walk.

Rio appeared last in sunglasses and a sunflower dress. She was the only Good Weather who had packed hiking boots, but the shades did little to disguise her hangover; Tom noticed how she drooped like a mushroom even though only he, Thames, and Bryce wore packs.

The route from the entrance to the park to the peak was four and a half miles each direction. They piled into Rio's Tahoe for the short drive to the entrance to Pine Bluff. The transit was bumpy, but brief. Outside, light poles and mile markers appeared to accelerate by, putting distance between themselves and the band of travelers.

The base of Pine Bluff had a parking lot and ranger's station. Outside, a ranger, who couldn't have been more than seventeen to Tom's eye, handed out maps of the park.

"Welcome to Pine Bluff State Park," he said mechanically as the group mustered past. "Please enjoy a complimentary guide courtesy of the Iowa Department of Natural Resources."

"We've already mapped our route," replied Rio holding up her phone, "but you are adorable. Are you complimentary as well?"

The boy chuckled and blushed.

"No, ma'am. I'm afraid I have to stay with the station."

"Pity," said Rio, and the boy wandered off to greet another group.

"If 'make some farm boy's day' was on your visit to Iowa bingo card, I think you can place a big X on that square," said Bryce peering back at Rio.

"I fear I would disappoint upon any deeper engagement, but I'm happy to remain a mysterious fantasy."

She paused for a moment.

"I'm just going to say it," said Rio. "I enjoy all of you, but I might request minimal talking on the trail. I'd love to claim that it's because I want to enjoy the incredible, transcendental beauty of the natural world. But the throbbing hangover headache is more front-and-center in my mind, both literally and figuratively."

"I think that might be more fitting, at least for the first leg of our journey," said Thames from the front of the pack. "Some due solemnity is in order. It will give us a chance to enter a spirit of communion with nature before the remembrance service."

Bryce shrugged. After his trek back from Shine or Rain with Thames, Tom was glad to be relieved of the obligation to converse.

The morning's abundant sunshine had given way to a more muted, cloudy afternoon. One brown squirrel chased another down the trunk of an oak, chittering madly. Whether this was territorial behavior or romance, Tom didn't have the Boy Scout expertise to know. For all the years he'd lived at the camp, Tom never grew accustomed to the wild.

He'd hiked this trail with Alle, but his more memorable recollection of climbing Pine Bluff was with Rain. Rain would sometimes orchestrate competitions among the Atoll staff to encourage them to complete a transcription or community pamphlet before a deadline. One of the most vaunted rewards was a hike with him in the nearby state park. Tom had witnessed the most zealous go without sleep for thirty-six hours or more in the hopes of winning an afternoon on Pine Bluff with the prophet. Since the work came naturally to him, Tom prevailed in one such contest without needing to endure that sort of deprivation.

On their "buddy hike," Rain guided the conversation as they mounted the increasingly steep slope. They kept a brisk pace. Rain spent a number of months in the wilderness outside Starved Rock, and he took great relish in identifying flora and fauna.

As they approached the top, Tom spied some luminous violet flowers growing in the crook of a dead elm. As they closed in, he saw their petals actually bloomed a deep red that flushed to lavender at the edges. He asked if Rain knew the name of the flower and if it was poisonous. Tom intended to bring one back for Alle. Rain considered for a moment, then responded, "I believe we are the first humans to ever examine this species of violet. We'll call it

Tom's Gift. And I command its poisons shall have no effect upon the faithful."

At first, Tom laughed, but Rain wore an unironic smile. He motioned to Tom to pick his namesake, waiting patiently. Tom did so reluctantly. For the first time, he truly doubted Rain. When they returned to Shine or Rain later that night, Tom washed his hands thoroughly, but he kept the flower in a glass by his windowsill until it wilted.

As the group approached the summit, Tom checked his cell phone. No new text messages, but no service either.

Anna had texted in the early afternoon for an update. No picture of her or Terra, which disappointed him. He responded that he was still undecided about his final destination, but planned to hike today.

From the moment Anna introduced his shy grand-daughter to him in his hospital room at Lutheran General, he knew Terra's name, Terra herself, was a repudiation of Anna's skyward gazing parents. It was Anna's way of saying, "Look at all you lost by letting yourselves drift away from the gravity of this planet, from me." Terra: her ultimate, irrefutable comeback. And when all Tom wanted was to leave the dead buried, her name made him love Terra all the more.

Pine Bluff ramped to a plateau that terminated in a steep precipice. When they reached the top, a family of three already occupied the fenced looking-post. A father carried his son piggyback, while his daughter stood on tiptoe to take advantage of the metal binoculars riveted to the guardrails. *If only I'd carried Anna like that,* Tom thought. He burned with jealousy.

Thames guided them a short way into the woods to an

outcropping with an equally pleasant view. At this distance, the camp appeared less ravaged by time. Tom wondered if, with his glasses removed, the camp might appear as it had on August 6th, the massacre blotted out completely. Perhaps, he'd see the fields lined with stalks, pickers like buzzing bees. Perhaps, their friends would be there waiting for them when they descended, the camp expunged of its new occupants: unencumbered weeds and vines.

The four sat in a circle, close enough to touch. Bryce drew a water bottle from his pack and passed it to Rio, who was bright with sweat. Tom extended his palms toward Rio and Bryce. They joined sticky hands. Breezes swam past cooling them from the hike.

"Yesterday I promised to join you in the Doxology of Water, and I am a man of my word," said Bryce, breaking the silence.

"Actually," replied Thames, "Tom and I chatted this morning. That recitation might mean more to me than to the rest of you. Something universal might be more appropriate."

Tom's mouth fell open.

"I'll give it to you, girl," said Rio. "You never cease to surprise."

"Rio taught the doxology to me last night so that I can join in," countered Bryce, "I don't mind."

"That's so thoughtful. Really," replied Thames. "But the doxology is not something meant to be recited lightly. We believe those words conform us to their utterance."

Bryce nodded respectfully.

For the first time since they stood examining the soccer field that morning, Thames made eye contact with

Tom. She could not veil her disappointment. Somehow this hurt made it easier to remember a time before she held stoic watch over the camp, when she was just Alle's best friend, a young woman who worked two jobs and longed for an escape and a purpose.

"Oh true scripture, may I be ever obedient to you," began Tom.

Thames shook her head. But she made no effort to stop him.

"Like the rain which washes the soil, saturate me till I overflow with truth. Clean me that I might be worthy of the estuary where I return."

Thames' alto voice overcame his.

"Like the flowing river, carry away the silt of my iniquity. Round me, till I am as you intend," she said.

"May those who go before us over the lip of the world, praise you in *Shamayim*," they spoke in unison. "Do not forget us in your majesty, and do not let us forget one another."

As they completed the final words of the prayer, a chill draft whizzed through the circle.

"I didn't know my dad well," said Bryce. "And I may never understand why he did all he did, why he sold the house mom and I lived in to keep Good Weather going. But I know exactly why he believed in this community."

Thames' face lit up.

Over the next few hours, the four memorialized their friends. Rio had printed off the names of those who died, and they took turns reading each. Sometimes one of them would tell a personal story before passing the list. They took their time. They let themselves be carried away. For a few hours, they were transcendent and open and kind.

Soon, the chrome sky was growing increasingly overcast. Behind them, Tom noticed the family of three had abandoned their post.

"I am all for finding closure up here," said Bryce. "But my phone says there's a weather alert issued for Eden County."

"Wait," said Tom, "you're getting service?"

Bryce nodded. Tom collected his phone from his pocket. He had bars and a photo message. He quickly input his password.

Are you in need of diet pills? it asked. Tom clicked the phone shut, ashamed by his own sorrow.

"I don't want to disrupt the solemnity, but I am gonna need a minute to eat," said Thames. She took out a granola bar and began munching.

"Ok," said Rio putting her hands out in front of her defensively. "No one needs to join me, but I plan to consume some of these." She divulged a sack of edibles from her bag. The translucent packaging read "Green Market, Denver, CO."

"I am absolutely willing to share, but I feel like I got raked over the coals on the whole vodka thing. Which, of course, is no one's fault."

Rio looked at Thames for any sign of distress.

"So, I want to be clear about three things. First, these delightful gummy cannabis treats were purchased legally in the great state of Colorado. Second, they are made from natural ingredients from the earth. Third, this is how I want to engage with this moment and those we've lost. But no one else is obligated to grieve my way."

Tom handled the phone in his pocket. No inkling of vibration.

"I'll take a couple," said Tom.

"Whoa, big guy. One should do it. I buy the good stuff."

Tom opened his palm, and she placed a large, red gummy bear there.

"I was planning to give this to you later," said Bryce, searching his pack, "but to assuage any doubts that I was coerced into signing, here is my release. Now drugs, please."

He handed an envelope to Rio who, Tom could tell, was working to contain her delight. Rio withdrew one for herself and another for Bryce, and the mourners consumed their treats. To Tom, the cannabis snack tasted like a normal gummy bear but with a more resin texture and, of course, an herbaceous flavor.

Bryce helped Rio up, and they dusted themselves off. Tom gave the valley below a parting salute.

"I would like one," said Thames, rising to meet Rio. She held out her hand expectantly.

"Are you sure?"

"The last thing I want to feel in this moment is left behind."

Rio reached into her bag, retrieved an edible, and handed it off. Thames quickly chewed and swallowed it.

Tom felt a droplet of rain collide with his sneaker. His cell jostled in his pocket to indicate that he was losing reception again. Then they were pressing back down the precipice, the weather at their backs.

CHAPTER 15

Roughly a mile down Pine Bluff, Tom realized what a fool he'd been to ingest the gummy bear. The creature growled from his innards, clawing as it flooded his system with THC. How could he have fallen for so obvious a ploy? The bear, by nature, was an apex predator. It savaged those who crossed it. Sure, it had been manufactured into a cuddly-wuddly toy, then, some years later, branded as a sweet, delicious treat. But this pleasant gummy visage masked its true character. The red gummy masque of death. How had he been so easily deceived into playing host? Where had this unimpeachable wisdom been mere minutes earlier?

In the ever more shadowy forest, he detected movement first at his six. Then dead ahead to the right. Several detectives lurked behind the largest oaks, studying and cataloging his smallest of tics. Would these minutiae provide clues? He always suspected the police had never given up their investigation. They wouldn't rest till he was behind bars.

Perhaps there had been no great prophet Rain.

Perhaps Tom pulled all the strings. The police were keen to prove his sole responsibility for the deaths of the whole Good Weather Community. The paparazzi had always been their agents in the whole endeavor, ferrying the police insider information, preparing for this moment when they would testify against him and he would be plucked from the human herd and thrown into a dark dungeon. Solitary confinement. His cell would make the boiler room of the Holiday Inn look like the Four Seasons.

The rain came down in sheets on their huddled entourage. Rio had extracted her phone from her bag and shined the flashlight along the trail. Bryce wobbled in front of Tom. The look didn't fit the young man. Usually, he moved with the surety of a loosed falcon. Thames still led the expedition, but she stalled each time the path turned, puzzling over changes in direction like an archaeologist reading some ancient cryptograph. Now, she stopped completely.

"Go right!" shouted Rio, the storm working to drown her out. "Turn right, and press forward. I can see the gap where the path widens out."

Thames turned left. She held her hand above her eyes to block the gusting rain.

"That doesn't look like the path!" shouted Thames.

"Of course it doesn't! You turned the wrong way," said Rio. She hurried to the front of their expedition and gripped Thames' shoulders, repositioning her to face the trail.

"Why aren't you at the helm, Rio?" asked Bryce. He was shivering. Bryce had put on a sweatshirt, but now it was soaked through.

"Good grief," replied Rio. "None of you can handle

your shit." She barged to the front, holding out the phone in a vain attempt to provide illumination.

Tom whipped around and was sure he caught a glimpse of Colorado, in bright blue shirt and cargo shorts, tiptoeing behind a nearby shrub. He grinned at Tom now.

There was no way that was real, he thought. It had to be the work of this damned gummy bear, his innocuous little pal with his THC payload. He imagined the gummy bear, cowboy hat in paw, riding a bomb through his bloodstream.

Tom realized he'd fallen behind the others and rushed to catch up. But what if it had all been staged? The suicide, the investigation, the documentary. When you considered it in the cold light of day, such a conjecture seemed preposterous. Sure. But memories could be planted with enough torture and conditioning. Certainly, *The Manchurian Candidate* had some basis in fact. Had he been waterboarded? Barraged with doctored pictures of his wife's death, of the bloody scene that night at Shine or Rain? Had the documentary been part of a long game to lure him back? No, the whole of it was too absurd, even if some afflicted part of him insisted upon its validity.

"Tom!" shouted Thames. "Why'd you stop? You're falling behind."

He heard her, but her words jumbled in his mind, scattered like letters in a word find. He was uncertain what act would satisfy their demands. Was that all that remained in his years ahead? The fleeting satisfaction of trying to please all these voices?

Rio shined her light on Tom. Bryce jogged toward him, but as Bryce ran, his right foot caught on a root. He fell forward. He braced his hands to keep himself from directly kissing the dirt. But he hit the earth with a *whump*. The fall looked bad, and Bryce assumed a crouching position, rubbing his scraped knee.

"Man, oh, man," said Bryce.

Rio rushed to examine him.

"I'm fine, I'm fine," he said. "Just skinned my pride."

"Let me at least get some Bactine on that," said Rio. "Who has my bag?"

"You didn't bring one," replied Thames.

Rio growled in frustration. Bryce moved to stand, and she worked to steady him.

"This never would have happened if you weren't off in your own dimension," Thames muttered, glaring at Tom.

"It doesn't do any good to turn on each other," shouted Rio.

"That's just the kettle calling the cat black," said Thames.

"Huh?" replied Rio.

"You know what I mean," she snapped. "Isn't that how you plan to make the big bucks once we're out of here? Getting us to turn on each other on the boob tube? To get a glimpse of how we might perform in your made-for-T.V. arena, what better than a moment like this one? Maybe you're recording our whole debacle here. This would make quite the lovely scene for your reality T.V. trainwreck."

"No," said Rio, examining Thames quizzically. "No one is recording anyone. But I am not engaging you either because, one, we're caught in a rainstorm. Two, you all are unreasonably high. Three, I think your sober self has let this issue go."

"Let me see your phone," said Thames. She futilely pawed at her.

Rio released Bryce, stiff-armed Thames, then backed up, swinging the light helter skelter. Tom shook his head, trying to gather his thoughts. The cloud cover in his brain began to lift even as the storm on Pine Bluff worsened.

"Knock it off," shouted Tom. "We've got one hurt and nearly frozen. And we're not even halfway down."

Thames squinted then pointed to the left of the trail.

"Shine the light over there," she said.

"That's not the path, hon," said Rio.

"Shine the light over there for just a minute, and I'll shut my trap and let you usher me out of here nicely."

Rio sighed but swung her cell around. To their left, a grassy outcropping gave way to steep crags. Between the muddy talus of each precipice, black-eyed Susans poked up, drinking in the early summer shower.

"Beautiful, no doubt," said Rio. "But all of us need to get out of this weather now."

Thames ignored Rio and raced toward the outcropping, carefully stepping around the flowers.

"What are you doing?" yelled Rio.

Thames took off her pack, unzipped the top, and began digging.

"Don't you remember what Rain said? He must have given that service a hundred times. When the *malak* dictated the true scripture to him, she resuscitated his black-eyed Susans. It was a gift, a promise of the renewal to come."

"I saw hundreds of those yellow and blacks on the way up here," said Rio. "You did too. It's a common flower."

"No, no, no," said Thames. "Coincidence is for the willfully blind."

She found what she'd been digging for and drew it out

of her pack: a sharpened bean hook. Tom felt like a spinning compass. Rio stepped back, but kept the light aimed at Thames.

"Whoa. What's the plan here?" Rio asked, her voice slow and clinical.

"Thames," said Bryce, "why do you have that?"

"Don't you see that these are all signs? The black-eyed Susans, the thunderstorm. I can go home now," she said. She smiled as she cradled the blade.

"You're not thinking straight," said Rio.

Tom edged closer to Thames. Bryce began to creep around the bed of flowers.

"I thought..." said Thames, "if we couldn't rebuild, you might want to come with me instead. Especially you, Tom." Her voice was soft; he could barely make her out over the storm.

"I can't yet. And you shouldn't go either. What about Anna and Terra? Wouldn't you like to meet them?"

He'd closed the gap between them to only a few yards. He'd lost track of Bryce. Thames settled the edge along her throat as though testing herself.

"I think...I think I'm finally worthy of *Shamayim*. I can control myself now, and Rain won't have to worry that I'll love him anymore. He won't be sick like he was at the end. We can be together."

"How about you come back to Des Moines with me? I'll introduce you to my girls," said Tom. He was drenched, but somehow his head felt like a boiling cauldron.

"I can't, Tom," she said. "This is the moment. I can still board the golden galleon. But I'll tell Alle—"

Then Bryce had both Thames' elbows locked behind her. Tom sprinted forward, attempting to loose the bean hook from her grip.

"You have no right!" shrieked Thames. She thrashed and howled. She elbowed Bryce in the nose and managed to get an arm free; but Tom pried the bean hook from her grip. He backed away. When he looked down at his hands, he felt a pang of disgust and self-hatred. The handle was sickeningly familiar. The inscription read *Bud's Agricultural Supplies, Burlington, Iowa, 2019*. She kept it all this time, sharpened it, packed it for the remembrance ceremony.

Thames was screaming and kicking at Bryce. Rio moved to back him up, but before she could intervene, someone shouted.

"Hey! What are you people doing?"

The youthful ranger from earlier and his superior lowered themselves from an ATV. The storm had muted their arrival.

"Our friend isn't well—" said Rio.

"I need you to drop that weapon right now," interrupted the ranger. His pistol was drawn, his eyes fixed on Tom.

Tom released the blade, which splattered in the mud, and raised his hands above his head. Bryce let go of Thames, who stumbled away with a huff.

"Danny, go collect that, please," said the superior. The young man hustled over, keeping maximum distance between himself and Tom as though Tom were radioactive, and fished the blade out of the mud.

"I'm a trained first responder," said Bryce. "This woman is under the influence of drugs which have impaired her judgment. We were trying to restrain her from attempting suicide."

The young man hunkered close to the older ranger.

The youth scanned over each of them, his hand shaking as he gripped the bean hook.

"I arrived to find you two restraining this woman while this fellow stood a few feet away with some kind of ceremonial blade. So, you'll forgive me if I don't take your word for it."

"Tell him, Thames," implored Rio.

But Thames remained silent, her face a veneer of bitterness and rage.

"Ma'am, is that true? Were you trying to hurt yourself?" asked the older ranger.

"My body is my own, and if I decide to cross to the opposite shore, that is my business," she replied.

The ranger made no attempt to disguise his befuddlement.

"We were part of Good Weather," said Bryce. "We're here to memorialize the people we lost."

"You're not helping your case," said the ranger. "We came up here to offer you a ride off the bluff, but that's not in the cards at this point."

He gestured to the ATV.

"We're gonna motor ahead on this, and you all are going to follow us at a quick clip down to the station. Danny will practice his driving, and I'll sit on the back with my hand on this holster. If I see something I don't like, the outcome will not be in doubt. We'll wait at the base of the bluff for the Sheriff. Do all of you understand?"

Each of them sounded off in agreement. They formed a line. Thames settled to the back, but Bryce and Tom moved to stand behind her.

"Stop fucking around back there!" shouted the ranger superior as Danny started the ATV engine. "Whatever you were up to ended the moment we arrived, and it stays that way."

CHAPTER 16

From the 2020 Netflix Documentary Series *The Good Weather* "Special Bonus Episode 11: Surveying the Damage"

(The documentary opens on a pudgy white man in his early forties. He wears a polo and jeans with a teal vest. The outfit seems designed to suggest he is hip, but neighborly. He sits in a dark leather chair in a room lined with shelves of books. Behind him, a tile patio gives way to a beach and then the Pacific Ocean. Waves crest and fall with the regularity of respiration.)

Don: "Hello, I'm Don Burlington, the director of *The Good Weather*, speaking to you from my home in Malibu, California. When we began this documentary a year ago, I had no idea the profound effect it would have not only on the community of Edenburg, but also on people around the world.

"I want to thank the executives at Netflix for their ongoing support of our project. I also want to thank my incredible crew who helped me tell the story of the Good Weather community and the warning implicit in it. And most of all, I'd like to thank you, our viewers, who have buoyed us ever onward in our quest to uncover the unexpected truths behind the largest mass suicide on U.S. soil.

"When we finished filming, I believed we had provided as complete a vision of the tragedy of the Good Weather community as was possible. But since the release of our show, new information has been unearthed, new figures have come forward. We want to share some of that with you.

"In May of this year, we revisited some of those haunted places and people we met while making this documentary. For some of us, including me, this meant reopening old wounds. But if any of us are ever to have true closure, perhaps we needed to reveal some of those traumas to you. That's why we're happy to share this bonus episode."

(The screen fades to black. The documentary cuts to handycam footage. The cameraman focuses in on Don behind the wheel of his SUV. He is driving down a rural highway. Deputy Lena Wan, much leaner than she appeared in the documentary, sits shotgun. The camera pans to a young man in the backseat. He rubs dry skin on the back of his hands. A caption identifies him as "Tim Alderidge, 'Gila,' Good Weather Member 2015-2016.")

Don: "We're here with Deputy Lena Wan and Tim Alderidge. Lena appeared in the documentary so you probably remember her, but Tim was behind the scenes. He was my fact-checker and all-around expert on set. But he's agreed to step in front of the camera today.

"Camp Shine or Rain is off-limits to the general public. The property was sold at auction a few months ago. Developers who purchased it plan to demolish the buildings and start from scratch.

"We've received a special permit from the Sheriff's Department and permission from Iron Works Development Co. to visit the former Good Weather compound before it's gone. We're inbound as we speak.

"Tim, how do you feel about passing back through those gates?"

Tim: (Takes a deep breath) "I've been mentally preparing for the last few weeks. The other night my wife, Callie, found me on our back porch totally comatose. I was supposed to be watching our nine-year-old son, Thompson, because Callie has been hard at work on a jewelry line that debuts at United Colors of Benetton this spring. I've been doing my best to support her because her work always inspires me.

"When she found me, I was in one of our lawn chairs. I was limp and unresponsive. She started shaking me because she was scared. Really scared. I came back to myself after a few seconds, but she hasn't been the same since.

"The prospect of returning to Shine or Rain has worked on me in ways I never expected. So, how do I feel about this road trip into the worst chapter of my life? Just like her, I'm terrified."

Don: (Reaching back to clap Tim on the shoulder) "You're a brave dude, and I'm so glad you're here to put some of this to rest." (Turns to Lena)

"Lena, your narrative of what you saw, heard, and felt that night at Shine or Rain was affecting not just for the audience, but for the cast and crew. Details you shared in our interview still give me chills. What are you feeling?"

(Don turns the wheel. There is the sound of gravel

crunching.)

Lena: "It's a little different for me since I live in the area. I take the highway around the soccer field at least once a week, but I avoid it if I can because...it feels prohibited to me, like the house of an abusive ex."

Don: "Does it feel like part of your psyche is prohibited too?"

Lena: "In a way, I guess so. Seeing the soccer field is like putting my finger in an electrical socket. And since Sheriff Mills retired, no one is around who remembers like we do."

Don: "It's lonely to bear that burden alone. It is." (Shifting the car into park) "I don't want to cut you off, but we're here."

(The camera bumps and jostles as the four pile out. A wooden, padlocked gate surrounds a ten-foot chain-link fence. The fence has only made the property more foreboding. Graffiti covers the gate including a red scrawl which reads "Leonard Fairbanks Burns in Hell." Lena draws out a ring of keys, finds the proper one, and removes the padlock. Chains rattle as the entry wobbles open. Don enters first followed by Tim, the cameraman, and Lena.)

Tim: "The fences make me anxious. They're a physical representation of what was going on here on so many levels: once you were in, there was no way out."

Don: "I know, but they can't confine you anymore. Don't forget that."

(The documentary cuts. When the camera turns back on, the three are inside Estuary Chapel, almost on the exact marks where Alle and Colorado delivered their lines during the orientation video.

Now the blue-tinted windows are boarded up. Several heavy wooden pews have fallen forward, one splintered down the middle. Crinkled leaves blow around the stage ahead of them. The carpet is wet and discolored as though it were the site of a sacrifice.)

Don: (Craning his neck around) "If ever there were a representation of Good Weather, it's this: a space once considered holy now in shambles. All Rain left in his wake was ruin."

Tim: "You never needed a watch to know when service started at Good Weather because, at the appointed hour, everyone would drop what they were doing and head here. The jobs closest to this building were plum because proximity meant you could snag the spots near the stage.

"Rain would come out and, oh, the whole community would go crazy. Like absolutely ballistic. Sometimes he'd speak for thirty minutes, but it wasn't uncommon for him to go on for an hour or two. And no one complained, even the people who'd been detassling all day and were starving. In fact, they cheered the loudest."

Don: "Do you remember who sat where?"

Tim: (Pointing) "The Atoll crew had front left. That's where Tom and Lisa Duncan posted up. And Katie Hunt was by the sound booth to the right of the stage. Rio was a grounds crew grunt, so she was somewhere over here." (He gestures to one of the dusty pews in the rear of the chapel.) "If anyone left for any reason, they had to sit in the back row for the first month. It was a severe punishment."

Don: "Where did you sit?"

Tim: "I did clerical work at the Atoll, so if you came to service any day of the week, you'd find me front and center. Kind of funny in retrospect, huh?"

(Don nods.)

Don: (Addressing Lena): "Tough to believe that what began here as an act of spiritual communion, or at least an attempt at it, ended in the massacre on the soccer field, isn't it?"

Lena: "I only visited this place once: when we were sweeping the grounds for any other survivors of the suicide. So, you didn't ask, but my feeling walking through the door? Nausea. When Sheriff Mills and I opened this place up, my hands were so stained with blood that they stuck to the iron doors. If ever there was some shred of the sacred, it was long gone by the time I set foot here.

"All I know is that the people who spiritually communed here ate a meal of Molly-spiked stew then took turns killing each other on the sports field next door. Their leaders fucked on a blanket, still covered in blood, then crawled into a Suburban to gas themselves. Not a damn thing spiritual about any of that."

Don: "Do you feel angry at the community, even though most of them were heavily drugged?"

Lena: "This may not be a popular opinion, even among the occupants of this room, but every adult who was at Good Weather on August 7th, made choices that led to their deaths."

Don: "And the children?"

Lena: (Her face stern) "The children...I can't think about that."

Don: "I understand. I do. What do you say we leave the chapel?"

(The camera audibly clicks off. When footage resumes, Don and Tim stand in the ruins of North Hall. The trunk of a fallen tree rests in the dining area having crashed through the roof. Crushed plaster and weather-worn siding hang from the ragged gash in the wall. The building is wounded and sick.)

Don: "Nature is reclaiming Shine or Rain in a hundred different ways. Do you feel any sadness when you see this, Tim?"

Tim: "Honestly, no. This feels like a metaphor for Good Weather. Rain did everything he could to cut us off from the world, to keep us from the people we once loved. But the world has a way of forcing its way in. That tree is simply a testament to how hopeless it was to seal this place away, and now, those of us left behind can see what a husk it really was."

Don: "Hard to believe one hundred and thirty-seven people ate their last meal in this room."

Tim: "I never reviewed the list of names. I never could bring myself to do that. But I'm certain I knew almost all of them. I ate three meals a day with them in this very room."

Don: "I wonder if—"

(Don is interrupted by the sound of something skittering across the floor. A piece of plaster tumbles and explodes. "Go, go," shouts Tim. Don shoves the cameraman towards the door. The camera clicks off. When the footage resumes, they are back in the SUV).

Don: "We hoped to stay longer, but we can't take any chances with the safety of our camera crew or our interviewees. Camp Shine or Rain has always been a dangerous place, and even without Rain, it seems that hasn't changed."

(Lena rides shotgun again. She looks pale.)

Don: "How did you feel being back at the site of the massacre?"

Tim: "It's sad. What other word is possible? When a community raises someone up on a pedestal like that and puts absolute, blind faith in their judgment, people get hurt. When there's no one left to hold that person accountable, this is what you get: a wasteland."

Don: "Lena, any thoughts? I'm sure this is difficult."

Lena: "There are people in this world who believe they can live above the fray, who imagine they're exempt from the moral judgments of everyone else. I see it all the time when we're called in for domestic disputes: you get these guys who think they're unquestioned king of everything. Those are some of the most dangerous people I meet in my line of work. It's incredible how much damage they can do."

(Don nods, his eyes fixed on the road. A final shot captures the shut gates of the camp. A single, sharp note plays from a violin. The documentary fades to black)

(A text block appears across the blank screen: "In the early summer of 2020, after this documentary aired, we received a call from Russ Stevens, Tom Duncan's brother-in-law. Previously, he had not responded to interview requests. But Mr. Stevens agreed to sit down with us at his home in Pittsburgh, Pennsylvania. He said that he had learned new information about Tom Duncan that he wished to share."

The camera comes into focus on a muscular man in his early fifties with a bushy beard. He wears a white dress shirt and tie. Neither seems to match him. Don sits across a kitchen table from him.)

Don: "Firstly, I want to thank you for meeting with us. I have no doubt that it's challenging to discuss your sister. As you can imagine, we have quite a lot of questions."

Russ: "That suits me because I got a lot of answers." (He laughs hoarsely.)

Don: "Tell me a little bit about your relationship with Lisa."

Russ: "Well, I wish I could tell you it was a rich companionship that had only blossomed further over the years. But truth is I hadn't seen her in twenty-eight years when she died. Not at Fourth of July, not Thanksgiving. And they sure as hell weren't sending Christmas cards from the cult. She was barely eighteen when that asshole, Tom Duncan, talked her into running away."

Don: "What memories do you have of her?"

Russ: "Well, one time when we was kids, she got up to make us breakfast. She was always thoughtful like that. She put this piece of bread in the toaster, but it was cut too thick. See, we made everything from scratch, bread too. So, she wanders off to do who knows what, but when she comes back the toaster is just spewin' black smoke." (Russ makes a volcanic motion.)

"I come rushin' in, still in my Spiderman PJs, and I start hollering that she's gonna burn the house down. She grabs the toaster and, I kid you not, chucks it out the window into the snow." (Russ grabs his stomach, hooting with laughter.)

"I figured I might as well start planning a funeral for her since mom had just bought that toaster over at Sears but a week ago. But Lizzy got the thing working again, she sure did. And she lit cinnamon candles all over the house to mask the smokiness. When my dad got home, he said the whole place smelled like a candy store."

Don: (Smiling) "It's those sort of childhood traumas that bond us together as siblings, isn't it?"

Russ: "I suppose so, I suppose so."

Don: "When you learned your sister had passed away and the manner of her death, how did you react?"

Russ: "Well, the news come on, and the 'caster said they had a late-breaking story about a cult suicide in Northeast Iowa, and I thought 'Oh no. Oh no, that's gotta be Lizzy.' My girlfriend Steph said I 'bout turned to a ghost right there on the sofa. But I just knew, as soon as that 'caster said it, that Tom and the rest of them assholes finally got her to walk the plank."

Don: "The people we interviewed from Good Weather, community members who left, some who had been there since the beginning, led us to believe that Lisa was something of a 'true believer,' that she lured Tom and others into the community. Are you saying that isn't accurate?"

Russ: "Now, I want to set the record straight on this 'cause I wouldn't believe Tom Duncan if he told me two plus two equals four. And anyone he hung around with, any of them people you interviewed, they are PBD, professional bullshit dispensers.

"Before she met Tom, Lizzy wasn't no cult freak. We grew up going to church like everyone else. But we weren't fanatics or nothing. Tom Duncan was one of these college boys who think they know the whole world, but they walk right into the gaping jaws of danger the moment they bounce out the schoolhouse door. I can tell you for certain that Rain or whatever his name was, he got his hooks into Tom, and Tom pulled poor Lizzy right along with him into that depraved lifestyle right up until it killed her."

Don: "Let me play devil's advocate here for just a second, Russ."

Russ: "Alright."

Don: "I think some folks watching might be skeptical. You declined our invitation to talk earlier. But now that, and I say this with all modesty, our program is one of the most popular in the history of streaming, you reached out. Can you tell me what's changed?"

Russ: "Well, it's a fair question. And the answer is 'quite a lot.' First, you gotta understand that with all that's happened, Don, our family name's been dragged through the mud. I'm lucky people know me, and they know all about my relationship with Lizzy because my sister Jenny? The one who raised Lizzy's daughter? Well, people egged her house, and someone left a spider in her mailbox."

Don: "That's awful. Absolutely awful."

Russ: "I appreciate you sayin' it. And we know you ain't the one who done it, obviously. But we've been careful from moment one since we found out what all happened out in Iowa. The whole family has, but we agreed it's time the facts get out there."

Don: "So you're a representative for your family."

Russ: "Certainly, certainly."

Don: "And what new information is it that you want to share with us?"

Russ: "Right, well, you gotta realize that this is really Jenny's story to tell, but like you put it, I'm a representative for my family."

(Don nods, urging him on.)

Russ: "In 2016, my niece Anna, Tom and Lizzy's daughter that they gave up to Jenny when they joined that cult, got pregnant. And all of us was so excited because it seemed like a new start for that side of the family, a chance for someone in that circle to have a normal life and do something good for change.

"We came out there for the shower and everything. But a few months before Anna's due date, she got sick with pneumonia or something like it. Doctors never did figure it out. And while Anna was sick, Jenny drafted up a note, begging, and I mean begging, them two to come back. Jenny wrote this heart-wrenching sentence, and I ain't gonna do it justice, something about losing two generations at the same time.

"Well, neither of them two ever came to visit, much less to stay. And after baby Terra was born, healthy and all, Jenny wrote Lizzy again to confront her. And this time Lizzy actually wrote back. She said she never got no other letter. And I am dead sure with all my heart it's 'cause Tom kept that letter from her."

Don: "I want to dig deeper, but first, since I know the audience is asking themselves, how is Terra doing today?"

Russ: "She is just the most lovely little child and absolutely healthy. But Anna's got a soft heart, and she let Tom move in just down the way."

Don: "How does that make you feel?"

Russ: "I'm terrified, frankly. I'm worried he is gonna take them both down that same dark road he took Lizzy and they ain't never gonna come back. That's why I'm sitting here, talking to you today."

Don: "How can you be sure Tom withheld that letter from Alle?"

Russ: "Look, I can't reveal everything, but I found ways to keep tabs on my sister, get information when I needed it. And I know, for a fact, that he withheld that letter to make sure she'd stay with him, that she'd stay loyal to all this nonsense he and Rain had cooked up over the years."

Don: "Has there been fallout from Tom moving close to Anna?"

Russ: "Oh, absolutely. He's poisoned her against me, one hundred percent. Since he showed up on the scene, she won't even call me and Steph, and she used to on the regular. Jenny doesn't wanna talk about it, but she's slowly losing Anna and Terra to his control. He's insidious the way he gets in people's heads, gets them all twisted up."

Don: "I'm so sorry for what has happened and what is still happening in your family. Is there anything else you'd like to say to Anna in the hopes that she might see this special?"

Russ: (Looking directly at the camera) "Anna, we haven't always been super close, but Steph and I love you. Tom may be your father, but he definitely ain't your dad, and he's a dangerous man. He's a man whose past is just gonna keep chasing him, 'cause some of what he done, no man can walk away from. Keep your daughter safe and get that Tom Duncan out of your life because as long as he's in it, there's always gonna be a blade pointed at your neck, too."

CHAPTER 17

Bryce, Rio, and Tom sat glum and wordless at the ranger station. Thames was sequestered above them on the second floor where the older ranger was interviewing her.

When they arrived, Danny kindly brought each of them a towel, but Rio was concerned about Bryce who shivered and shook uncontrollably. Danny said the cabin had heating pads and a space heater and offered to let him use them. While Bryce raised his body temperature, Danny sat in a chair near the stairs, opposite his three unwanted guests.

In this moment, what Tom Duncan wanted was to talk to his granddaughter. To be home. These desires pressed on him with the intensity of a freight train. They were the intense and immediate instincts of a scared child.

"My sole job was to avoid any PR disasters," said Bryce, shaking.

"I imagine it isn't much consolation," said Rio. "But no one who examined the facts of what happened up on Pine Bluff could blame you, even the PR department of the world's largest seed company. Thames is not a variable you could have planned for."

"You didn't do me any favors, dispensing your little grief care packages," whispered Bryce angrily.

"You're absolutely right," replied Rio. "I should have anticipated that Tom would dawdle in the rain which would cause Thames to go totally haywire when she saw a patch of generic flowers. If only I had remembered to check her itemized list of pack contents to see if she brought her sharpened bean hook. Silly me!" Rio wagged a sarcastic finger at herself.

"Well, when you chuck lit dynamite into a fireworks factory, anticipate explosions," replied Bryce. He turned his head away.

"For real? Seriously?" said Rio incredulously. "I am responsible for some *serious* toxicity in my own life, and I've taken a torch to more relationships than I can count. I'll own up to all of that. But this? I gave you a choice. I all but obliged you to sign affidavits before I put one, just one, of those damn bears in each of your palms. Don't lay the brokenness of this whole situation on me because I tried to help in some small way."

"Your assistance is much appreciated," said Bryce, with a snort.

"I recognize you're being sarcastic, but I'm going to accept that," replied Rio.

Tom slapped his hand on the end table. It rumbled and shook. Danny shot Tom a dirty look.

"That kinda white boy, power bullshit doesn't work on me," said Rio, her voice raised now.

"Did neither of you notice that we're not cuffed and headed for processing? The sheriff's deputy is inbound, and if we get our heads on straight, maybe we can all walk out of here without assault charges," whispered Tom.

"Police in these Podunk towns aren't known for their restraint," replied Bryce.

Danny glared at him from across the room then leaned back in his chair.

"I am going to ditto Bryce," said Rio.

"I wish you wouldn't," replied Bryce.

Tom cut in before Rio could retort

"Take it from a guy who had abundant opportunity to analyze the motives and procedures of police up close and personal: no matter how racist or angelic they might be, what moves the needle for them is perception. And I guarantee you that the last thing that the township of Edenburg wants to announce is that anyone from Good Weather set foot in their county, much less that they started a mountainside brawl. The county certainly has no desire to reveal that one particularly zealous party was all set to commit suicide on public land."

Rio rolled her eyes.

"If we play our cards right, behave like rational human beings, maybe the sheriff's department quietly drops the whole matter in exchange for our immediate departure and a promise never to return. We get off with a lifetime banishment. We go home, forget all of this."

Bryce stood up and paced. The cords of the heating pads tethered him to a small radius. He looked like a robot from some black-and-white sci-fi film.

"Quiet banishment?" he said. "I would totally take that and run."

"Sounds like the only way to take it," replied Rio.

"Hey!" shouted Danny, his voice cracking. He motioned for Bryce to sit down.

Then the door popped open. Danny jumped, and his chair clattered to the floor. A deputy in a rain slicker stepped through the doorway.

"It's fine. It's just me," said the cloaked figure.

"Hi, Deputy Wan," he replied, gathering his composure.

She unbuttoned her slicker, looking around at the motley crew.

"Where's Keith?"

"He's upstairs taking a statement from the other woman, Katie. We worried they might fight if we kept 'em all in the same place."

"You two both did a nice job. Tell Keith I want the carbon and original of that statement."

Lena Wan hung up her coat and removed her muddy rain boots. She moseyed over to the stairwell.

"Keith?" she yelled, craning her head up the stairs.

"That you, Lena?" came the muffled voice of the ranger.

"Sure is. You want to bring that one downstairs?"

There was the sound of creaking boards, then Keith descended followed by Thames. She had blankets piled atop her shoulders and sipped a cup of coffee. She looked far better than she had on the mountain, though not well.

"We're going to do a bit of musical chairs," said Lena. "Tom Duncan."

He looked up.

"You're coming upstairs for a chat, and Katie can have your seat. Keith, you and Danny keep an eye on these three? Also, why is he covered in heating pads?" she motioned to Bryce.

"I figured we'd let him warm up on account of getting soaked through," replied Danny.

"I appreciate the good care you both have taken of these folks. Danny, you've always had the best manners."

Danny blushed.

"Thanks, Mrs. Wan...I mean Deputy Wan."

Lena began trudging up the stairs then motioned for Tom to follow. He dutifully got to his feet.

The upper level of the station was surprisingly cozy. A woven maroon rug covered the floor and antique maps of the park mounted under glass adorned the room. A taxidermied deer, positioned to be eternally grazing, stood near the landing. The deputy took a seat on a couch and pointed to a bench across from her. Tom obliged. He was ready to concede to anything.

"You want to start with the conversation I want to have or the conversation we need to have?" she asked.

Tom considered.

"If we don't start with the necessary conversation, the elevator tune of anxiety will play on loop in the back of my mind."

"Fair enough. Please give me your rendition of what happened on your way down Pine Bluff."

"We're in Edenburg because--"

"Fast forward," interrupted Lena. "You're in a small town. There is no flying under the radar. Assume I know everything before the descent."

Tom recalibrated, trying not to reveal his own nervousness. He would need composure if this didn't play out as he hoped.

"We were coming down the bluff when the rainstorm hit. We followed the trail, but it got dark. Katie began arguing with Elise because Katie was under the influence of substances which impaired her judgement."

"Were any of the rest of you under the influence of these substances?" asked Lena. Tom noticed she had not picked up her notepad.

"In the interest of full disclosure, yes," he said and sighed.

"Well at least you're honest even if you're stupid," replied Lena. She leaned back on the couch.

"Fair. Can I continue?"

Lena extended a hand to welcome this.

"Katie saw flowers that she believed to be a sign that she should commit suicide. And we learned she had a sharpened blade for that purpose."

"Is that the item that the rangers confiscated from you?"

"Correct. Bryce, the man warming up when you came in, and I wrestled it away from her."

Lena put out a hand for him to stop. She rose and walked over to the stairwell. She whistled to Danny on the landing below.

"I believe I saw a coffee pot on when I arrived. Can one of you make us a couple cups?"

Tom considered protesting that he was not a coffee drinker, but a voice told him that this was more about ceremony than taste.

She carefully retook her place.

"Are you or your friends a danger to yourselves or anyone? Look at me dead-on when you answer."

"No," replied Tom without missing a beat.

"Is Katie Hunt, or Thames as I think you call her, a danger to herself or anyone else?"

"Uncertain and no."

"I was really looking for a solid 'no' on both counts. If

she harms herself here in Eden County, we will find ourselves with a series of front-page stories that'll do a lot of hurt. No one wants to relive Good Weather."

"Neither do any of us," said Tom. "What if we agree to leave town tonight? If Katie is going to be a problem, she doesn't have to be yours."

"I didn't take you for a mercenary," she said. She sounded disappointed. Tom worried he'd slipped up.

"I think in the clear blue light of day, she'll be fine. I really do. But I also believed our evening wouldn't end with a police interview in this beautifully-appointed ranger chateau. So, I can't bet everything on what Katie Hunt may or may not do."

Danny ascended the stairs and placed steaming mugs of coffee in front of both of them.

"Good man," she said.

Danny hustled away. Lena took a sip of the coffee and signaled Tom to do the same.

"I can't put any of you on the road out of town until I'm sure you are clear of whatever you took up there. You sleep. You wake up, drink some coffee. Tomorrow, all of you are gone."

"Absolutely, absolutely," agreed Tom.

"Two conditions attached to this. One, the rangers will dispose of that blade. It will not be returned to Ms. Hunt."

"You would be doing us a favor."

"Two, I am going to forget all of this happened. Keith and Danny are going to have a bout of amnesia as well. But I am friends with Sylvia Dennis. If I hear that any one of you are still on hotel property by nine a.m., my memory and theirs is going to become a whole lot sharper about the events of this evening. Do you understand this?"

"I do," said Tom, not trying at all to veil his relief.

"I'm going to present these instructions to the others then release you to sleep off whatever is in your systems. Is one of you able to drive?"

"Elise is stone cold sober. Not an issue."

"Okay, that works for me."

Tom got to his feet, but Lena remained and took another sip of her coffee. He hunched back down.

"I'm glad we got that part out of the way. I want you to understand that nothing either of us says next will affect the decision I just made."

Tom was puzzled, and this, more than anything, made him nervous. Perhaps he was still suffering from lingering paranoia. Was the villainous gummy bear wreaking havoc somewhere in his stomach? He silently cursed it.

"I figured you recognized me when I came in, but I believe you have absolutely no clue who I am, do you?" said Lena.

Tom eyed her up and down. He took a drink of coffee hoping to buy himself time. His brain was a vacuum.

"You're sure that nothing I say now will have any bearing on what we discussed earlier?" said Tom.

"You never even watched the documentary? The documentary about the event that completely shattered your life?" said Lena.

"I lived it. I didn't care to relive it, surprising as that may sound in the context of tonight's events. I'm only here...I'm only here because people I care about needed me. I needed them too," he said. Hearing his own words caught him off guard.

"I meet most people on the worst day of their entire lives. But you are the only one I met on the worst day of my life, too," Lena said.

Now, suddenly, he understood.

"You were there. You were at the camp when they—"

"I was at the camp, but I wasn't on the field when Alicia and Ralph found you. Sheriff Mills asked me to disable the wind siren. I saw the bodies, and I, I'm the one who found Rain," she said. The words overflowed out of her.

"I almost watched that documentary to see that one image. I wanted to know how Rain looked at the end. But I couldn't because..."

Tom trailed off.

"I get it," said Lena. "Are you asking?"

Tom said nothing.

"He looked pathetic, like a rabid dog that had been put down."

Tom struggled with what to say. Some part of him burned with a curious pleasure that he realized had always been just below the surface.

"I appreciate you telling me. If you're looking for some kind of apology—"

"No, no," she said. She tapped her fingers on the desk. "Now that Sheriff Mills retired, no one will talk with me about it. No one who was there. The EMTs, most of them moved on, and the rest go to therapy to unload all this stuff. The shrink route never worked for me, feels like talking to a block of ice.

"I thought doing the documentary might exorcise whatever was living in me, but Don Burlington...what a piece of work. I'm glad you didn't see it. No one should have to relive that night and the days that followed. I'm sorry I did."

Tom felt at a loss.

"I think maybe there is something you want to ask me?" he tried.

"When I was driving over here, I had a burning question, but now that I'm sitting with you, mostly I just want, for two seconds, to be with someone who was there, no matter your role in it," said Lena.

"It sounds like it might have done you some good to hike to the top of Pine Bluff with us," he said.

He recognized, suddenly, that Lena Wan, in no uncertain terms, had survived the massacre too. But just barely.

"Maybe in another life," he said.

She considered this and did not nod or shake her head. She lingered for a second as though she might say something more. Then she left the table.

"I'm going to gather your friends and explain things. If Ms. Hernandez is of sound mind and body, she'll drive you back to the hotel. I recognize you needed to make your peace here, but now," she said, "you need to let us make ours."

CHAPTER 18

The yelling and crying did not begin until they reached the hotel.

The group boarded the SUV, Bryce still shivering. Thames sat shotgun. Rio drove carefully and capably, minding the speed limit. They blasted the heat.

To Tom, the interior of the vehicle may as well have been the vacuum of space. The oxygen felt thin and denatured. And a cold, irredeemable blackness permeated the vehicle. What was five minutes, in this wholly relative space, felt like hours.

When they reached the hotel and entered the elevator, Rio instructed them to change clothes then assemble to discuss a system of accountability for the next day.

"Five minutes, in my room," said Rio.

A ding signaled their arrival, and they slouched away soggy and bedraggled.

Tom changed clothes and vainly attempted to turn his phone on. He plugged the phone into the charger and held the 'on' button, but its battery was too low. The illuminated clock read 9:30, so too late to call Anna and Terra anyway. It was all he wanted in this moment.

When he opened the unlatched door to Rio's room, Bryce perched on the edge of one of the twin beds. Rio paced back and forth in the small runway between the table and wall. Thames sat in a chair, her damp hair wrapped in a towel. She hugged one knee to her chest. Tom shut the door behind him then leaned against the armoire beside it. In the mirror, the avatar of pure exhaustion, a man with storm clouds hanging below his eyes, gazed back at him.

"What did you tell her, Tom?" demanded Rio without pausing her repetitive motion.

"I told her the truth," replied Tom.

"You admitted to a small town deputy that your friend gave all of you edibles, that you were all high as kites, then Thames attempted to kill herself?"

"Look," said Tom, "I told her we were high, but I didn't tell her where the drugs came from. I didn't even tell her what we took. And she didn't care! No harm done, and she's going to keep her mouth shut."

Rio resumed pacing.

"We're not sitting in a holding cell," Tom said incredulously. "No one is preparing charges. We get to walk away as long as we never come back. Seems more than fair."

He glanced around at the three poor souls in the room. If he were not so exhausted, it would have been easier to feel sorry for them.

"I'd like to believe no one is self-centered enough to ruin this by sticking around for a second spin down memory lane, but we also just dodged an attempted murder charge. So, I am not willing to operate on good faith at present. We meet in the grand ballroom tomorrow morning at nine," said Rio.

"You're all being hyperbolic," muttered Thames.

Rio stared at her, mouth agape.

"Hours of silence, and when you finally step to the podium, that's your line? You've gotta be freaking kidding me!" shouted Rio. She flopped backwards on the bed.

"What were you thinking?" demanded Bryce. "Bringing that blade with you. Why do you still have it?"

"My body is my own, and if I want to go home, to be with the people we lost, nobody decides that, but me," said Thames.

"Why? Because some storm clouds blew in? Because you saw a patch of flowers?" said Bryce.

"Coincidence is for the willfully blinded," replied Thames, pulling her other leg to her chest.

"You almost broke my arm the way you struggled. You were out of control. Don't you know we care about you? What's so urgent after death that it can't wait?"

"If you believed in the true scripture, you'd understand," retorted Thames.

"Would you shut that shit off for, like, a second?" yelled Tom. "I feel like you flipped some switch after we hit Pine Bluff, and now it's all just jargon and dogma! Earth to Thames?"

Rio stuffed her face into a pillow and softly cried. Thames glared at Tom. She opened her mouth to speak, but Tom bellowed over her.

"You talk like Rain, but you're not him! And that's wonderful news because he died like a sick animal. Rio, you wanted to know why it took so long to negotiate our release? Because that poor deputy was one officer on duty the night of August 7th. She's the one who turned off the endlessly blaring wind siren. And she got an up close and personal view of the ugly fate of the Good Weather community. She's the one who found the suicide SUV and the sick scene inside.

"She's a victim. She probably has more in common with us than either of her ranger pals because after whatever happened to her at Shine or Rain, she's never going to be the same."

Thames jumped up. The towel fell from her head, her wet hair whipping her back. She tried to push past Tom, but he grabbed her shoulders. He wasn't sure why, but he needed her to understand.

"You need to hear what I'm telling you. She saw Rain. After he was dead. She said he looked like a euthanized mutt. That's your great guru! A dead, naked dog, bathed in disgrace. And he took my wife, your friend! Everyone we loved!"

She forced Tom back into the armoire, burst through the door, and slammed it behind her.

"Your tact and subtlety..." said Rio emerging from her pillow. She put her fingers to her lips and made a kissing motion. Her makeup ran down her cheeks

Tom used the counter to pull himself to his feet. He caught a glimpse in the mirror as he did. What he saw was wet snake brought low by its rage at the world, at himself most of all.

"Whatever moral high ground you believe you hold, I promise you, I just did more good in thirty seconds than any program you produce will do in a whole season," said Tom.

Bryce shook his head.

This was hopeless, Tom realized. He'd rescued them, but they were children, swimming away from their life preservers, all of them enamored by some glimmering mirage in the distance. It was pointless.

"Get your heads on straight and pack your bags," breathed Tom.

Then he shoved past the door and stormed into the hallway. No one followed.

Back in his room, Tom dug frantically in his pack for Angela Downey's card. He stuffed his fingers in the pockets of polos. He turned linings inside out. He ran his arm beneath each twin bed then shook his bag. He felt like a TSA agent scouring a carry-on. Had an x-ray scanner been available, he would have employed it, lead vest or not.

Who in their right mind ordered black business cards? And what company fabricated such nonsense? A hex upon them. He kicked the bag across the carpet and slammed his hand against the comforter. His wrist struck the frame, and he winced, holding it in pain.

He rechecked every garment, hurled a pair of jeans at the wall. They flopped in a sad, bunched heap.

He must have lost it somewhere on the hike. He envisioned the card pinioning from his jacket pocket into a pile of leaves. Lost forever. Probably picked up by some storm-wrecked bird to rebuild its nest. A magpie or a dove. Perhaps the bird would put it to better use.

He slumped against the bedframe. He surveyed the mess. Then a car passed in the parking lot and briefly flooded his room with light; he spotted the filigreed edge tucked under his bag. He seized it greedily.

He snatched his phone, yanking it from the wall jack. The phone's usual animations played in slow motion, until the illuminated backdrop, him and the girls at a Mexican restaurant, came into focus. Then a new message from Anna. It read, *Haven't heard from you tonight. Concerned. Call before bed.*

He glanced back at the clock: 10:15. He pulled up her contact and dialed.

When she answered the phone, her voice tired, but glad, he struggled to respond.

"Quite the day, I'm guessing?" she asked.

"You could say that."

"You'll have to tell us all about it some night."

There would be more nights. He practically glowed with warmth.

"I'd like that. I really would."

She paused. "Terra just went down, and I think I'm going to crash too. I'm glad you called, though. She's been asking about you."

"I missed both of you," said Tom.

"We miss you too."

Some warning system blared in the back of his brain, told him how unfair his next question was. He overrode it. He'd been through too much today not to take his shot. And he was willing to gamble, maybe be rebuffed, for some glimmer of hope

"Have you given any more thought to what we talked about before I left? I was hoping a little absence might make the heart fonder?"

"Dad, you know that I want to say 'yes,' don't you?" she said. "It breaks me when Terra checks to see if grandpa is keeping a watchful eye on her from the couch. She doesn't understand why you aren't here, and she asks about it over and over. And what can I tell her? But she's a three-year-old and has no idea what's best for her. Even if you've mended all your fences, if you've miraculously bandaged your deep wounds, you won't turn this around overnight because every day is going to bear with it another angry woman in the park, another small town photographer keen to catch up with alleged cult murderer Tom Duncan. You're a powder keg in a matchstick hamlet. You need therapy, and you need time. And so do we. Maybe me most of all."

She sounded breathless as she finished. The words rang in his ears. He sagged against the bedpost, defeated.

"That came out meaner than I intended," she sighed. "But you've cornered me after I've had Terra all day with no help."

"No, I understand. I do. I want to take the heat off our family. I may have found a way to walk clear of all this, to tell my side of the story," he said. He waited for her response. He felt like a corpse.

"That's great. Really it is. I'm not sure what more to say. I think it's best if we talk tomorrow when my head is clearer. It's not fair to you or me, engaging like this."

They said their goodbyes, and she hung up. He sat numb for a moment, listening to the restless hum of the air conditioner, the chirping of a night bird on a nearby branch, a group of friends hurrying by, rallying for an outing at the casino.

He thought of a submarine. Where once he'd been safe and warm inside the hull of the ship, now he silently witnessed the lives of others through portholes like these.

The temperature felt fatally chilling. And around him, no prospect of rescue. Just the crushing weight of all that water above, bearing down on him with neither malice nor mercy.

If he'd known what lay ahead, he could have stored up those moments with Terra, somehow slowed time down to absorb every second. He could have resisted sleep and counted her infant breaths as she curled in his arms. He wouldn't have forgotten the popsicles in the park, would have bought fifty boxes just to get more red ones.

He reopened his phone and texted Angela, *This is Tom Duncan. I'll leave with you tomorrow. Send details.*

He lay against the bedpost waiting for the face panel to illuminate, for some immediate recognition of his willingness to give up his last modicum of hope for a private life. A few seconds later, a reply from Angela scrolled across the screen with instructions. He scanned the information. He recollected his clothes and possessions scattered across the carpet, resetting each in its proper place in his bag then rezipping each compartment and checking under the bed and dresser. When he'd prepared his baggage, he noticed Alle had appeared, her legs folded beneath her on the table.

"I don't want you here," he hissed.

"It's not fair to blame me for what she did. I'm not your wife," she replied.

"No, you're not!" shouted Tom. "All you have is her face, so it's pointless to talk to you, to ask you what kind of monster lurked just beneath it, isn't it? You can't explain to me why I meant so little to her. I don't know you. Never did. AND. I. WANT. YOU. OUT!"

He seized the alarm clock and hurled it; it detonated

against the wall. Wires and shattered bits of plastic fell to the carpeted floor in a heap. A faint smell of battery acid wafted from the detritus. When he blinked, the ghost was gone.

He dimmed the lights and seated himself in the chair where he'd begun the day as a voyeur of the homeward bound wedding goers. He closed his eyes. Then for the first time since he woke handcuffed to a hospital bed in Waterloo, he allowed himself to break down and weep.

CHAPTER 19

When Tom passed through the ranch-style gates to the Silver Horse Pub, Thames already occupied a place at the bar and was scrutinizing a martini. He attempted to reverse course through the swinging doors, but Thames rolled her eyes and waved him over.

She kept her gaze fixed on the drink as he took a stool.

"I have zero desire to continue our conversation from earlier. You're a real jackass, and you were wrong. But I could use companionship. It's too close to midnight for any more verbal brawling anyway. If you wish to sit here, you will accept all of this as fact. We will agree that you are sorry. Does that work for you?" she asked.

"More than you know," he replied. He waved to the bartender who dutifully acceded and grabbed the soda gun for his rum and Coke.

"You planning to drink that or prepare a professional inquest into its properties and motives?"

"I haven't yet decided, but I have several P.I.'s awaiting my call," replied Thames.

"Wait a minute," replied Tom. "Did you play off a joke?

Where has this woman been all weekend?"

The bartender returned with his drink, and he raised a glass in a silent cheers. But Thames didn't join him.

"Patrons told me I was funny when I tended bar at Raccoon Saloon, but I suspect every bartender is a comedian if you're drunk enough. And people who came in the saloon were there to do business. No amateur hour. So, I was the funniest gal in town."

"I always thought that was something of a one-eighty for you, the leap from bartender to personal attendant."

"Oh, that was easy. I listened, I anticipated, I made the day more bearable. They were nearly identical jobs, but as an attendant, instead of tending to a bunch of lousy drunks, I tended to a man I admired."

"But to go from pouring drinks to a dry lifestyle, that still seems like a big leap."

Thames peered at him, puzzled.

"Alle never told you I was in recovery, did she? I started AA four months before we met Rain."

"Really?" Tom said. Had he somehow erased this from his memory? Certainly, he and Alle talked about Thames, especially in those days, but she had never mentioned this. "I guess we were more physical beings back then, Alle and me; we exchanged elements other than words."

"Congratulations," replied Thames, "you've officially squelched any regrets I had about all these years of abstinence."

"You're welcome," said Tom with a laugh.

"AA didn't work for me, but in the spirit of fairness, I never gave it a good faith shot. I never bought in. I just let the bandwagon drag me behind it. But Good Weather, Rain, our people: those were reasons to stay sober. And since the end, I've kept it up in the hopes that we could revive that community. Maybe more honestly and openly this time. That ghost of a chance kept me from driving to the liquor store and filling a cart to capacity."

Tom pointed to the martini in front of her.

"Maybe I should take care of that for you?"

"Sometimes you need to toss a bad idea around for a little while, feel it in your grip before you let it fly."

She lifted the glass by the stem, making jet engine noises. She hovered it over the bar before returning it harmlessly to its coaster.

"Why shouldn't I anyway? What's left to lose?" she asked.

"You just saw," replied Tom. "There are two people one building over and another right beside you who were willing to face felony charges and go toe-to-toe with one cop and two of the fiercest rangers in Iowa just to keep you breathing on planet Earth."

Thames covered her mouth, coughing and laughing all at once.

"Those two tender hearts wouldn't even be a match for Yogi and Boo Boo."

"Ok," began Tom, wagging his finger in the air, "firstly, that is an unfair metric because it is clear that the forest service has never been and will never be a match for either of the bears in question. Secondly, you are, as the kids say, dating yourself with that reference."

"Terra doesn't watch Yogi the Bear?" Thames inquired.

Tom couldn't help but grimace at the mention of his family. He took a long drink of his rum and Coke. He thought of their *Aristocats* afternoon and tried to measure out the weight of his little granddaughter in his arms.

"That bad, eh?" she asked.

"When you are young, and you talk about following your dreams, about giving up everything else, it makes total sense because the everything you have isn't much: a crappy apartment, a couple shelves of books, a cat if you're particularly lucky. But you get older, you have a child, and you see the scope of what everything could be...it's like looking over the edge of a tall building. The sheer distance is staggering."

"How much is Anna like Alle?" Thames asked.

"Shockingly similar, especially considering that she never knew her mother well. Why?"

"Alle was horrible at dieting. She would carry around those awful magazines in her purse with 'the latest medical research' on blah, blah, blah, by Doctor John Smith of the American Federation of Medical Medicine. You remember that, right?"

"I was a victim of the culinary exploits arising from her dietary madness more than once," replied Tom. He allowed the faint memory of burnt spinach pie to surface, but tamped it down before it could do any damage.

"She would ramp herself up for these mighty endeavors to improve her general health and wellness. For a few days, she'd be a zealot and banish all sugar or refuse to eat anything not composed of primary colors. But then she'd spy a burger stand at just the right moment or someone would pass her a dessert menu," said Thames.

"The siren song of cheesecake," he replied.

"She could lash herself to as many masts as she wanted, but cheesecake would wait her out. And what made her truly a marvel is that she never whipped herself over it. Not for a second. It was all part of the tidal force of her personality. She had the rare capacity to forgive herself completely.

"Only two things ever seemed to stick: Good Weather and you. If your daughter has one-eighth of Alle's DNA, she'll open the door for you sooner than you think. You're her cheesecake."

Tom wanted to believe this more than he wanted his next breath to fill his lungs.

"What makes you so certain? Isn't it different when it's your father?"

"No. She lived decades longing for you to walk back through the door. Then you did, and it turned her world upside down. Now she's scared, and she's having trouble sorting out how all of this works together. But she's trying to envision a life big enough to hold her, Terra, and you. She wants to know you won't walk away again and hurt Terra like you hurt her."

"I wish I presented Anna with my tall building metaphor," he replied.

"Yeah, well, you hadn't realized that truth until this very moment. That's why we weekend away in these scenic towns where all the residents hate our guts: perspective."

She rapped the glass with her finger and lowered her nose to sniff the glass.

"I do believe I am about to drink this," she said and grasped the drink by the stem.

Tom felt panic. He'd been bluffing when he offered to throw her fate to the winds in the ranger cabin. He knew it at the time, but he felt it viscerally now. He put his hand over the martini, dampening his palm.

"I tell you what: all I own in the world is stuffed into a

duffle bag. I can barely afford my next round, but I will proffer you anything I own to let me finish that for you."

She released the stem. She tapped her finger against the counter.

"I believe you have something worthy of that exchange, but you aren't going to like it."

"Whichever one of my dirty articles of clothing or worn copy of *Anna Karenina* you want, I guarantee it is worth seeing you walk out of here still sober."

She set her index finger against her lips.

"The hotel minions really screwed me in that game of Single Query because I had a burning question for you. I felt like I needed to ramp into it. When the agents of hotel propriety showed up, round two was cancelled, and I was out of luck. But if they hadn't, I would have mustered the gall to ask. I intend to unleash my banshee of a question now."

Tom ran through a catalog of every topic he dreaded and cross-referenced them with what Thames knew. There was significant overlap. But he suspected she was not lying about her willingness to default on her sobriety.

"I accept your terms," Tom replied, even as he lamented his own willingness.

"When I dragged you back to Shine or Rain, I was forcing you to face one demon, and I admit this question grows out of the same impulse. Tell me honestly: I always suspected Alle and Rain were sexually involved, but did you know before the end? And if so, why did you stay?"

A thousand sounds filled the room—the clack of billiard balls, the squirting of the soda gun, the jukebox playing Tom Petty—but suddenly they were all silent.

"You're such an asshole," he said. He wanted to slam

his hands on the bar and to cover his face in shame in the same moment. He allowed himself the brief pleasure of envisioning shoving over the stool and crashing through the swinging doors.

"Hey, hey," she grabbed his shoulder and straightened him till he met her gaze. "I am not asking for me. You need someone else to carry this. It's been festering inside you too long. And you know what happens in Single Query stays—"

"This isn't a game," interrupted Tom. "You can't ask me to pull shrapnel out of a wound this deep."

"I am here to help you. And this is the bonus round," replied Thames, "so you aren't bound by the usual rules. But if you don't answer, I am going to see where that martini takes me."

She reached for the glass.

"Stop," said Tom. He threw back the dregs of his rum and Coke then signaled to the bartender. While Thames waited silently, he snagged the martini and chugged it in a single pull.

"I consider that guzzling a legally binding contract," replied Thames.

He waited for his drink to arrive then slowly began to speak.

"After you left, Rain became even more secretive than he had before. He locked himself in his quarters at the Atoll when he wasn't giving a service. So, anyone who needed his attention had to come to him.

"In July, after he announced the end was coming, Alle told me that Rain asked her to be his interim attendant. I was excited for her. She said she would be at Atoll all hours of the night for 'prayer sessions' or 'organizational meetings.' I didn't care.

"Since so many other community members had been hallucinating, not sleeping, passing out at odd moments, I figured she and Rain were tending to safety concerns. It sounds stupid when I say it now.

"In late July, after service one night, Rain pulled Alle aside. He spoke to her for a couple minutes. He was talking really fast. She agreed to whatever his request because when he walked out ahead of her, he was smiling. I asked what was up, but she said it wasn't hers to share. So I backed off.

"I woke up that night around two, and Alle was gone. Between the late hours and my own nausea from drinking the water, I just had it. I threw on jeans and a t-shirt and marched up to the Atoll. I planned to tell Rain that no matter his spiritual condition, he needed to correct course because vanishing at all hours had all the appearances of impropriety. The community was going to gossip. I didn't think anything was really happening, or maybe I wouldn't admit it to myself.

"I arrived at the Atoll, but the building was totally dead. But I could see from the window the lights on at Estuary. I figured Rain and Alle were practicing for service the next day. You and Rain used to prep in Estuary sometimes, right?"

Tom looked to Thames for some confirmation. Some part of him still hoped he was wrong, that all of this made sense. But Thames shook her head in resignation.

"When I got to the reconciliation room, the side door was unlocked," Tom halted, hoping not to continue, not to unshutter Pandora's Box. "I don't...I don't think you want to know what comes next," he said.

"I can guess, but I need to hear it from you."

Tom coughed. He ran a hand through his grey hair.

"Like I said, the side door was unlocked. They weren't even being that secretive. And there was blood, good grief. Bloody handprints on everything. The door handle, on the floor...you couldn't even walk in without stepping in it. They were just laying there naked on the chapel rug. Rain still had his leg on, and they were laughing. It felt like they were mocking me. And when they saw me, it took a minute for it all to sink in."

"I don't...I don't understand," replied Thames, closing her eyes. "Who was bleeding?"

Tom nodded.

"I figured one of them was hurt, and I was yelling. I couldn't process all of what was happening. Alle grabbed one of the towels they were laying on, put it on, and ran over to me. That's when I noticed the goat carcass over in the baptismal font behind the stage. All I could think was 'it's so wasteful, that whole animal...and in our sacred space.' And both of them were talking all at once about being gripped by the spirit. Then Alle was shouting that nothing had happened."

Thames put her head in her hands. She held up a finger.

"I'm sorry," said Tom. "I'm sorry you have to know, too."

"I'm not," she said. "I needed to."

Tom longed to stop but it was all coming out like the pus from a sore.

"Alle tried to calm me down. She laid her head on my shoulder. I think, in retrospect, that maybe she was high. But I brushed her off, and I was walking away. But Rain grabbed me and spun me around. I shoved him, but he stood his ground. He shouted that I had two choices: to forget this one moment and travel with him aboard the golden ship to the next shore or to let this ruin everything right before I was so close to the end. He told me that if I said anything, he'd excommunicate me in front of everyone.

"Alle protested, but he gave her a stare. It was the one time I believe I ever saw the true face of Leonard Fairbanks. And if I was a bigger man, if I didn't feel some sick urge to cling to the flotsam of my life, I would have walked away right then. But, in that moment, all I wanted was to take Alle home and wash off what they'd done together, to forget any of it. So, that's what I did. And she let me believe it could all wash away. I lived in that single moment of shock until August 7th."

Thames said nothing and just stared at her knuckles. She growled then screamed. Tom snapped from his terrible reverie. The bartender approached.

"You two are done for the night," he said.

"Oh, I'm not fucking drunk," snarled Thames. The bartender did not respond, but continued toward the console.

"Hey, hey, cool down," said Tom and placed his hand on her shoulder.

She brushed off his hand and shook her head.

"Don't you get it?" she said, her voice still raised.

"Tell me, but just do it in a lower voice. Any trouble right now is more than we need."

"This is why he sent me away. I was just a casualty of his need to fuck someone else's wife. He knew he couldn't do it while I was on site because I'd know and call him out.

From the moment Rain stepped into our lives, he had this weird dynamic with Alle," replied Thames.

"I don't think any of this goes back that far—"

"I know this is a moment where you're unloading baggage so awful that it would break anyone's back. I should just be listening, but I can't. I'm sorry. I heard five million pick-up lines at Raccoon Saloon, and it's dawning on me that maybe Rain just came up with the very best one. But it wasn't even for me. That's never been clearer than now."

Tom sat stunned.

"If ever there were a testament to your goodness as a person, it's your failure to recognize the obvious scheming that went into all of this. Alle always knew how I felt about Rain. Then a month before the end, she tells me 'maybe I should share with him how I feel.' That's where that whole narrative began. Then it was spinning in my head like so much laundry, and...and."

Tom's mouth felt dry and woolen. Thames rose from the stool and began putting on her coat.

"I didn't mean to—"

"You don't have to defend yourself," replied Thames. "And nothing happening right now is your fault. You did the right thing, being honest with me. I just need some time."

To Tom's total shock, Thames leaned down and kissed him on the cheek. Then before he could respond, she was past the doors and into the now empty lobby.

CHAPTER 20

At 8:53 a.m., Tom programmed his phone with directions to the small airfield Angela had indicated in her text message. He'd slept poorly, his dreams horribly alive with images of the goat bled in the font. It reared up and bahed at him; it trotted across the stage, its gore soaked mane like the flag of some diseased country.

Tom had arrived at 7:30 at the booth in the grand ballroom that had been their deployment zone during Operation Kitchen Infiltration. He'd flipped through his tattered copy of *Anna Karenina*, hoping to steady his racing anxiety. But Tolstoy was a poor palliative. He mostly counted words and listened to the awakening caws of birds in adjoining trees as they roused from sleep.

At 8:57, Rio, wearing a dress shirt and slacks, a surprisingly formal selection for her, slid in across from Tom. She carried no luggage, not even her purse of infinite capacity.

"You already stow your gear in the car?" he asked.

"I did," she replied.

He fiddled with his watch.

"The others are cutting it close. This is exactly what I wanted to avoid."

"Actually," said Rio, "Bryce left twenty minutes ago, and Thames left some time during the night. We're the only two remaining."

Tom felt wounded. The last twenty-four hours had been tough, but he assumed they knew that this was how families worked—sometimes you squabbled.

"What I said last night, I was in a bad place. And now I have to leave it like that?" said Tom.

"You'll see them again, soon," replied Rio. She swallowed hard.

"What, at the next reunion? We're too old to leave anything unsaid. When will—"

"Tom," she said, "Thames is in the hospital in Waterloo. She's in a coma."

Tom studied her face for any sign of a joke. If so, it was an awful setup and delivery.

"No, no, no," said Tom, "I just...we had drinks, well, I had drinks at the Silver Horse almost till midnight."

Rio snatched her cell from her jacket pocket.

"Do you know how many drinks she'd had when she left? Any information I can provide the doctors will help."

"She hadn't—" he said, but then stopped short. How long had that martini been sitting there? Or was it the first of many? He hadn't smelled alcohol on her breath. Had she grifted him to get the truth about Alle and Rain? No, he didn't suspect it, but Thames was a consummate performer, so it was possible.

Rio put her hand on his wrist, and he stirred from his internal debate.

"Bryce is on his way to Lutheran General. He was with

me when the hospital called—"

"How did the hospital even know to call you?" replied Tom. "None of this makes any sense."

"Realize that I want to share all of this with you, but if we're going to avoid issues here in Eden County, we need to leave now. I wish we could ride together, but we, neither of us, can leave our cars here."

Her voice was calm and soothing. *She will make a good T.V. show host*, he thought.

"I can't go," replied Tom, "I mean, I can't go to the hospital. This woman, Angela Downing, from *60 Minutes*, she chartered a flight for me to New York. I was going to tell viewers my side of things, remind them I was a victim."

He realized how pathetic all this sounded. He saw the shadow of a jealous thought pass over her. She struggled to regain her composure.

"I can't deal with this right now," she said. "I'm incredibly angry at you, and I think it's a dick move."

Tom remained statuesque, frozen by shame.

"I hope you change your mind about the release. It might be our last chance to be together before we're all as gray as you," she said. "Now stand up."

He got to his feet, and she took his arm in hers and led him through the lobby, past the sliding glass doors, and out to the parking lot. He did not check if Sylvia Dennis lurked behind the checkout counter. The grandeur of the hotel now seemed a rebuke of his own sorry life.

When they exited the building, he spied a squad car in the rear of the parking lot. Lena sat on the hood, hunkered over a cup of coffee. Rio waved to her in hyperbolic fashion. Lena returned a firm salute.

"I believe this is where we part ways," said Rio.

"You must know I want to be with you at the hospital. I never planned for any of this to happen," he replied.

She wrapped her arms around him.

"You are a good guy sometimes, in spite of yourself and in spite of all the shit we've been through," she said. Then she released, "Until next time."

She piled into her mighty white SUV while he loaded his bags into the rear of the car. She did not wave as she passed.

He started the Sonata, idling slowly out of the parking lot. As he turned right into traffic, he watched Deputy Wan hop off the hood and open the door to her squad car. The Good Weather survivors were leaving Edenburg. Lena's wish was granted. Soon contractors would bulldoze the last of their wayward home. The soccer field where the poisoned victims of a madman leapt off the edge of the world would be roughed beneath a dozer blade until nothing remained. When he considered all of this, Tom remained mercifully numb.

Highway 20 roped around fields of white stalks and billboards with adorable babies admonishing drivers to choose life. To Tom's mind, the problem with all of these ads was that they never explained what sort of life one should choose.

A brown-tailed hawk circled in the distance, hunting rodents foraging by daylight. The scenery was window dressing, and he raged at himself for focusing on anything but Thames. But it was these thoughts he could quantify and understand. Soon he'd be far away, literally miles above. Perhaps he'd spot Rio's massive vehicle in the parking lot. Meanwhile, Angela would go on about the format and schedule.

Another mile, and the babies on the billboards grew increasingly earnest and judgmental. Didn't it matter what kind of life? The kind where you kept your feet on the ground, didn't walk out on your daughter, didn't abandon your sick friend in the hospital? When he put it like that, it was simple. But the monkeys on his back were so weighty; they stalked him at all hours, hoping to hurt the people he loved with camera flashes, angry words, something worse. He let the thoughts spiral into a tornado.

She wants to make sure you won't walk out again, Thames said.

No. He couldn't pass through the cabin door to Angela Downey's charter flight. He couldn't put that distance between him and his family. He pulled onto the shoulder, clouds of dust kicking up around the Sonata. He rerouted the maps program to Lutheran General Hospital. The babies on the billboards remained beyond the dust cloud. But now, somehow their faces seemed softer, more cherubic, and he hoped that they approved.

After following directions from a couple of nurses congregated by the snack machine through multiple labyrinthine passages, Tom found his way to the intensive care unit on the fifth floor. The sound of heart monitors brought home the reality of this moment. Between his time at the bar and sleep, he purposefully hadn't given himself the tools to dissect this new grief. But now, he was without excuse.

Bryce sat by himself on a wooden bench, his back

pressed against the wall. Tom joined him, and Bryce flinched in surprise. Then he put a huge hand on Tom's shoulder, squeezed and released.

"Rio told me you were gone," he said.

"I imagine she supplied other choice words about me as well," he replied.

"Several."

"Scolding babies talked me out of air travel," replied Tom.

"Well," said Bryce, "at least you're here for the right reasons."

"Where is Rio?"

"Coffee machine. Rio and I met for a walk. That's when she got the call. We were planning to grab breakfast, but that never happened, obviously. And she was ravenous even before we left the hotel."

"Which room is Thames in?"

"Still in isolation. They had stabilized her when we arrived, but she had a seizure. So, the doctors took her back to run more tests."

Bryce rubbed his eyes and blinked, evidently, trying to adjust to the fluorescent lighting.

"You look like you need sleep," said Tom.

"Whenever I get home, I plan to outsleep Rip Torn," replied Bryce, yawning.

"I believe you mean Rip Van Winkle, but if you wish to outsleep American film actor Rip Torn, I think that may be healthier than going after Van Winkle's record anyway," said Tom with a laugh.

Bryce managed a smile.

"About last night—" said Tom.

"That's like nine million miles away from my mind

right now, honestly," replied Bryce. "I know you and Thames made up last night anyway. Whatever she did, none of this is on you."

"Wait," said Tom, "I figured Thames got in some sort of accident."

Rio reappeared carrying coffees enough for two. She passed by him briskly and handed the cups of coffee to Bryce. She then turned and hugged Tom with all her might. He could barely breathe.

"What you gave up to be here: it was worth it," said Rio.

She simply looked tired.

"Sorry," said Rio, backing up, "I get so emotional when I'm hungry. Have any doctors come out?"

"No," replied Bryce, "but a hunger strike won't hurry the news along. I saw a breakfast place advertised on our way in. It's just one floor down. I can keep watch. You'll just be a flight of stairs away."

Rio gave him an uncertain look.

"Hey," said Bryce, "it's not pure altruism. Bring me something back, please."

A doctor in horn-rimmed glasses emerged from a private door. He spotted Rio and walked toward the group.

"Your friend," he began, "she's back in a comatose state, but she's stable. She's intubated. I won't be able to stay long, but know that we're doing everything we can."

"Will we be able to see her soon?" asked Rio.

The doctor shook his head.

"If she permanently stabilizes, and that's a big if, it's going to be very touch-and-go. It'll be a while before she'll be able to have visitors. But we're a long way from that now. I need to get back, but we'll keep you updated."

With that the doctor about faced, flashed his badge at the electronic lock, and reentered the ICU.

"Go eat something," said Bryce once the doctor was gone.

Rio didn't argue. They left both coffees for Bryce then made their way to the elevator.

When Rio used the term "hungry," she meant it. She ordered practically the whole restaurant. Their food arrived, and she attacked her pancakes, sawing them with a dangerous intensity. Once they had some food in their systems, Tom addressed the elephant.

"Why was Thames an hour away? What happened to her? Why did the hospital call you?" he fired off.

"Some of this is necessarily conjecture, but I can tell you what I know," said Rio. "The second question is easiest to answer, so I'll start there. Thames is suffering from acute alcohol poisoning. Some time after she left the Silver Horse, she drove to The Gin Rummy, a late night liquor store in Waterloo. The owner said she started filling up a cart. When she got to the front, he asked her if she was having a party. She didn't respond."

"Oh no," Tom heard himself say. Suddenly, he floated over his body. He wanted any escape from this moment. But this horrible dream ensnared him. The goat toddled before him attempting to verbalize in spite of its slit throat. All the anger inhabited him, all the betrayal. It was all he was. How many times would Alle poison the people he loved?

Rio continued: "He saw her load everything in her car, but she didn't go anywhere. A few hours later, he noticed her vehicle was still in the lot. He went out to look. Thames was passed out in the front seat, but she'd thrown up everywhere.

The owner called for EMTs immediately. He wasn't sure she was breathing, so he tried to open the door, but she'd locked it. He grabbed one of the stock boys, and they broke the glass right as the ambulance arrived."

"Thames knew what she was doing," said Tom.

"That's why Waterloo," said Rio as she pushed away her empty plate. "She didn't want any of us to suffer because she killed herself. She could control that much."

"She's suffering because of what Alle did," said Tom to no one in particular.

Rio looked at him, puzzled.

"I don't follow," she said.

Tom scanned the room to find their waitress. The cheery, colorful lights adorning the restaurant seemed to have a weight of their own. Their waitress stood at the hostess stand, chatting with another server. The other server attempted to disguise her interest in their table, but the two whispered in hushed tones.

"Can we have our check?" he inquired in a wavering voice.

The two servers continued chatting, ignoring him.

"Excuse me!" Tom yelled. The whole restaurant looked up.

"Holy crap, they'll get to it when they do," laughed a gruff man in a hunting jacket two tables over. His buddy leaned back and said, "Wetback and four-eyes." The two laughed loudly.

"Don't engage them," said Rio, but Tom was on his feet.

"Don't you know I'm famous, big guy?" said Tom. "I'm

the cult messiah. Watch the documentary. I can kill someone with a single word. Wanna see?"

"Shut your mouth and sit down, or I'm gonna put you down," said the hick in the hunting jacket.

"Tom," said Rio, her voice fraught with anxiety.

Attracted by the yelling, the manager, a spindly wisp of a woman, emerged from the kitchen.

"I have no idea," she shouted, "what is wrong with you, but you'll sit down, pay your bill, and get out. If you don't, I'll call security."

But Tom's focus was on the tubby hick. His shaved scalp glinted. Did he have a metal leg too?

"Our friend upstairs is in the ICU because I cast a spell on her. I drove her insane with a simple incantation. Wanna know what I told her? It'll only take a second."

Rio opened her purse, withdrew her wallet, and slapped several bills on the table.

"Ok," said Rio, "we paid. Let's go."

"Bryce said he wanted us to bring something back, and I intend to," said Tom. He edged toward the two men, tears streaming down his cheeks.

"You're crazy," said the hick. He stood. His friend noticed and uprooted himself as well.

"What does a lard ass like you have to do besides watch T.V.? If you saw the documentary, you'd know I let some sick asshole run my life then fuck my wife. I'm a big fuckin' mess," said Tom. He was inches from the hick's face.

The hick laughed uproariously. His buddy joined in.

"Wow," said the man. "You must be a total pansy."

"You didn't even eat your muffin," replied Tom. "Mind if I take it?"

Tom reached for the muffin, and the hick tried to push

him. But Tom sidestepped and cuffed him in the ear. The hick went down, cracking his arm on a nearby table.

His buddy swung at Tom, but Tom kicked the table at him and caught him in the diaphragm. The friend grabbed his midsection, and Tom socked him hard in the jaw.

The tubby hick cowered on the floor. Tom picked up the muffin.

"No one takes anything from me! You hear me! Not my wife, my reputation, my dignity! From here on in, never again!"

"We need to leave right now," said Rio. She grabbed Tom by the shirt, and the two hurried away to the stairwell. Tom hoped to feel vindicated, but as he mounted one flight then another, everything inside him was gray.

CHAPTER 21

At the top of the stairs, Rio seized Tom by the front of his jacket and shook him hard.

"GET. A. GRIP," she directed. "And give me your jacket."

Tom peeled off his windbreaker. He was ashamed and deflated. Why had he waited so long to pour out his anger at Rain for taking Alle or at Alle for allowing it? In the end, who had she even been to him? He tried to summon her ghost so that he could shriek at it, hurl it over the railing, watch it tumble bloodlessly down the cement landings. But the specter wouldn't reappear, not now.

Rio fished in her purse and emerged with a cap: "Misfits" embroidered in monstrous letters.

"A more appropriate use of branding there has never been," she said and slapped it on Tom's head. "I need you to understand two things right now. First, you have to pull it together. Whatever has busted out of its cage, whatever monster is tearing loose inside you keen to wreck everything and everyone in its path, get it back in its pen. Do you understand?"

Tom nodded. The adrenaline had worn off.

"Second, whatever happened at the bar last night, whatever words passed between you two, Thames' condition isn't on you. You didn't speak some sorcery that inspired her to double fist Wild Turkey in the parking lot of a liquor store. Whatever minefield we lay for ourselves is ours to walk. It's taken me years of therapy to figure that out. I'm saving you the expense. But what you do from this point on, that is on you, too. Don't compound tragedy with tragedy. Now gimme that damn muffin."

She released him, and he handed off the muffin to her. Rio pressed on the crash bar, and they piled out of the stairwell. They located Bryce where they'd left him. He appeared slightly more caffeinated.

"The doctors said they don't know for sure, but they think she'll pull through. She's in the recovery room. We can see her through the window."

Rio passed Bryce the muffin, and they hurried around the corner.

Thames was being wheeled out by an orderly when they arrived. Her arms hung at unnatural angles. The dressing gown barely covered her long frame. A breathing tube dove into her throat, and a swarm of IVs led from her arm to machines which counted down or up in a language unintelligible to Tom. Her eyes were closed.

"I wanted to see her," said Rio. "But not like this...she is such a proud person."

Tom remained mute. *I'm sorry. Don't die,* he thought and propelled the words toward Thames' prone form. He noticed an officer in uniform approaching, and he lowered the brim of his cap. But she walked by toward the orderly's station.

"Don't worry," whispered Rio once the officer passed. "I suspect the manager never called anyone, and, I hate to tell you this, but you're a generic looking dude."

Bryce eyed them both up and down then considered the muffin.

"Should I even eat this?"

"Are you opposed to muffins acquired through violence?" inquired Rio.

"You have successfully talked me into holding out till lunch," said Bryce. He spotted a trashcan behind Tom and tossed the pastry in.

After a few minutes of stoic surveillance, Tom retreated from the window. He repeated Rio's wisdom, but the guilt pecked at him like a hungry bird. His secret was like a virus that Alle had cultivated, and in digging into the past, he'd unwittingly loosed the germ on Thames.

"She can't hear or see us, and we're just clogging up the hallway," said Rio. "I am an amateur at hospital visits. Is there a private room available to guests?"

Bryce picked his brain for a moment.

"Not really. At least no rooms where we couldn't be chased away by someone with more official business. But I saw some lawn chairs by the loading dock."

"I refuse to open this," Rio removed a large manila envelope, "on a smoky loading dock."

Their names were written on the front and, after each, their phone number.

"Has to be private," said Rio. "I don't have a clue what's in here, but I am doubtful Thames intended us to open it in the glorious light of day in front of the probing eyes of the public."

"We walked by a prayer room on our way up," said

Bryce. "Who is going to burst into a prayer room unannounced? I can stay behind and retrieve you if there are developments. While you were gone, I was in some sort of limbo between the waking world and sleeptown. Felt pretty good."

"She seems stable now. And whether one or more of us stays here, doesn't change that," replied Rio. "Plus, your name is here too."

The prayer room was quiet, luminous, completely inoffensive and uninspirational. Someone had arranged black, matte folding chairs before an unadorned wooden altar. The door to the room had no lock, but the room was windowless and, based on its pristine condition, clearly received little traffic.

"I've put together that the envelope is the answer to my remaining question from the café," said Tom.

Rio nodded and pointed to it. Her name and number appeared first.

"Thames was clutching this in the car. I'd like to believe I was given priority because of my consistently reasoned and responsible behavior," said Rio.

"You carry merchandise by a band whose claim to fame was dressing up as punk rock monsters," replied Tom and pointed to his head.

Rio considered this for a moment then nodded in agreement. She smiled, and for a moment, Tom remembered the young woman he had known so many years. The needle of this brief happiness pierced his second skin of guilt and sadness.

Rio opened the clasp then drew out a handwritten letter and a series of smaller envelopes. She set the envelopes on a neighboring chair and unfolded the document.

Rio began to read aloud:

Dear Good Weathers,

I'll skip the old clichés because the whole point of our community was to live differently from the rest of the world. I intend to abide by that even in death.

The letters here were going to be my parting gift to you, but I think we can agree that nothing about this weekend went as planned. I hoped to restore your faith, but maybe I've lost some of mine. Not in the true scripture, but certainly in its prophet. I'm scared disappointment is all that awaits me on this shore, not in any of you, but in myself.

Before the end, Rain asked some members of the community to write letters to people they loved. The idea was to provide a testament to the Good Weather faith that others could share. I don't think anyone was aware of the letters besides the authors themselves and Rain. Before he died, Rain put those letters in an envelope and mailed them to me. At the time, I believed he trusted me alone to see that this correspondence was delivered. Now, I suspect it was a final reminder of how much control he held over me, even once he'd crested the falls.

But I never delivered them. Not out of defiance, but because it was a way of holding onto a piece of Good Weather that was mine alone. Selfish, yes, I know. But it's clear to me now that I've not been well nor is there any prospect of reaching that illusory plateau of wellness in this life. As such, I'm entrusting the task to you. There are a handful of other letters to former members. I've left them to you in my will.

My time on this coast has been marked by incredible honors and journeys out of bad weather and into good. I count knowing all of you among those honors. I love each of you deeply. Thank you for fording that bluff with me one more time before I walked off it. I will see you on the sunnier coastline.

Thames

Rio managed to reach the final paragraph before she choked up and had to stop. Eventually, she steadied her voice and continued. After the last word was out, she carefully refolded the letter and placed it in her pocket. Tom yearned for more. Somehow, it felt reassuring to know Thames had been hurt as deeply as he was; he wasn't alone as long as Thames' letter ran on, as long as she clung to life.

"If no one objects, whatever happens today, I'd like to hang on to that," said Rio. "I suspect I might want it in the dark to come."

She gathered the stack of envelopes from the chair beside her and dispersed them like Christmas gifts.

"Obviously, Thames' letter was for all of us, so it made sense to share it out loud. But some of these might be too much. Do we read them as a group? I'm asking because I don't know myself," said Bryce.

"I don't mind sharing whatever is in here," said Rio, "That's not a value statement on whatever you all want to do. That is just me, and I'm happy to be the crash test dummy by going first. It's secrets that tore us apart at Good Weather. They're still doing it. I'm done living that way."

Tom turned his letter over in his hand while she unsealed her envelope. He considered setting it down so that he could focus wholly on Rio's own surprise mail. But he couldn't bring himself to release the simple envelope. He was all impulse and response now. All raw nerve.

Rio unfolded the lined paper, scanned the page, and began to laugh.

"What?" demanded Bryce.

"It's...it's from Colorado of all people," said Rio.

"C-O!" shouted Tom. "What a goofball!"

Tom was surprised by his own laughter, and Bryce chuckled along, willing to ride the euphoria train.

"Ok, knock it off, you scoffers," said Rio, wiping away a tear of laughter. "This is supposed to be a reverent occasion. Bryce, you're second most responsible; you need to be Thames' proxy and police this stuff."

Bryce affixed a menacing scowl, and they all got one more chuckle.

"Ok, here are the words of C-O himself," she began.

Dear Rio,

How the heck are you? Let's get the big awkward out of the way. Yup, by the time you get this, we'll have crested the falls. I'm scared and excited, like how you feel when the roller coaster cart is about to hit the top of the hill, and you can see the big drop ahead.

Rain asked some of us to write letters to Good Weather members who aren't going on the golden galleon to the next shore. I chose you because, well, I miss you, girl. The days haven't been the same without you. I miss our open mic sessions in the kitchen. You remember our carrot microphone? We should have returned that thing to Radio Shack because the recording quality was crap.

Rio paused to giggle and wipe away a small tear.

I gotta be serious though. Maybe I am a little scared. I don't know what the other shore looks like. But I believe it's gonna be beautiful from everything the true scripture says. And we'll all be there together. I wish you were going with us on the boat, because I always felt brave with you. But I'm sure you'll arrive soon enough. That's not some spooky prophecy from your otherworldly friend, either. I just believe you'll get there.

Until then, don't buy all the B.S. you hear on the news. I'm sure they'll make it seem like we're a bunch of psychos and not a community of people who all believe the same thing and who don't want to journey through this life alone. Haters gonna hate.

Well, I got shit to do. Be good, girl. But not too good.

Your Friend,
C-O

Rio smiled and carefully replaced the letter in its envelope.

"That one I'll hang onto for the light after the dark

days," said Rio.

Bryce tapped his letter against his knee. Rio rose from her chair and seated herself beside him.

"I have no authority to tell you what to do, but I think you should open yours," said Rio.

Bryce stared at the letter in his palm.

"There's the version of this that I want to read, and then there's the actuality, the same way there was the version of my dad that I needed and then the man himself," he said.

"I think if you don't open it," replied Tom, "you're going to have two ghosts instead of one. Better to know. I speak from experience."

Bryce ran his finger over the seal. He paused and then ripped. He handed the letter inside to Rio, and she opened it.

"You sure?" she asked.

"Yeah, go ahead."

Bryce,

When you read this letter, I and the rest of the Good Weather community will have departed this shore for the next. Likely, our choice will make little sense because you are still slave to the faulty logic of this world. I blame your mother for that poison.

Perhaps you imagine the pandemic raging across the world and the increasingly erratic weather have nothing to do with one another. But coincidence is for the willfully blind.

Bryce got to his feet and stood with his hands on his

hips. He faced away from them.

"I can stop," said Rio.

"No," replied Bryce, his tone firm. "I want to hear the whole thing, the whole lotta wisdom dad's got to share."

Rio did not immediately resume; Bryce shook his hand in impatient consternation, and she continued.

I have little to say. I hope you turn from your wickedness toward the true scripture before the end. The malevolence is without mercy for those it catches in its maw. May the true way be illuminated for you.
Atlantic (Gerald) Benson

When Rio finished reading, silence lay over them like a thick layer of dust. Bryce motioned for her to hand him the letter. She reached forward and placed it in his fingers, and he gripped the letter by the top, shredding it piece by piece then savaging each shard until the correspondence was little more than pulp.

Bryce punched wildly in the air. Tom stared on with admiration.

"Couldn't you stop being a total self-centered asshole for just one second?" Bryce shouted.

"Shhhh..." said Rio walking toward him then turning him to face her. Tears darkened his cheeks. She gripped the back of his head and hugged him. When she let go, he calmed.

"I'm sorry," said Rio. "I'm sure Thames didn't know that letter would be so hurtful."

"It's worth remembering that your father was drugged in addition to whatever else was happening with him," said Tom. Part of him wished he could say the same for

Alle.

"Doesn't matter. It's no one's fault but his," said Bryce, sitting back down. "I've learned that a thousand different ways—as his son, as the inheritor of his bad financial decisions. It just doesn't make it any easier."

Rio joined him and laid her head on his shoulder.

"You think that's from Alle?" asked Rio, pointing to Tom's envelope.

"I'm pretty sure," said Tom.

"You can choose to keep it sealed," she said. "No one would blame you."

But he'd known from the moment Rio passed him the letter that he intended to see its contents.

"Nah," he said, breaking the seal. "I shattered Thames' world last night. It seems only fair to let her return the favor. I'll tread the minefield."

As Tom withdrew the note, he recognized the familiar, bubbly cursive he read a thousand times on reminders tucked into his messenger bag, on love letters hidden beneath his pillow, on their marriage license.

He leaned forward, his hands on his knees, and read.

Dear Anna,

Congratulations on your new little girl. Until recently, I received letters from Jen. She told me about the pregnancy. She wrote that you were in grave danger of losing your daughter, and I want you to know that I prayed for you. I rejoiced when I heard the baby arrived, though I am sorry that Jen stopped writing afterward.

It was too much to tell your father about your

troubles. You'll have to forgive me that. But I knew he would rush to you because his heart is a marshmallow, and there was still so much work to do here at Shine or Rain before the end.

I hope you like being a mother. I should never have attempted the task. But even when you were just a kicking little bundle inside me, I loved you so jealously. I still do, even if the work here at Good Weather has taken me away from you.

I know I've made sacrifices that seem impossible to understand. I wonder if that isn't the greatest cruelty this world has to offer: that some callings must be greater even than motherhood or fatherhood.

And now, your father and I are preparing to journey further and farther away. I doubt the world will last long once we've crested over the falls, but I wish you and your daughter peace in what time remains. We'll wait for you on the other shore, and until then, may the true scripture be ever apparent to you.

Alle

Tom finished reading, and Rio lifted her head and reached into her purse, digging for something.

"I'm sure," said Rio, "I have a crow in here somewhere that Don Burlington can eat after his little expose with Russ Stevens carries him into court for slander."

"Can we give Tom a second to process before we start salivating over the possibilities of legal plunder?" said Bryce.

Tom ran his eyes over the words, feeling each like the

beads of a rosary. Here was the wife he remembered, the face she showed to the world. What had been true? He felt some comfort that the face he knew was the face she longed to show, the made-up, motherly visage, his consummate partner. Had she truly desired to be with Rain, to bathe in blood? He couldn't be sure, but she didn't want to be remembered that way.

"No, Bryce, it's fine," said Tom, resetting the letter in its envelope. "I thought it would break me, opening this. But right now, I'm relieved. I think, unconsciously, I believed Alle should have survived, not me, because being a parent, a grandparent would have come easier to her. I was wrong. I've been trying to live up to an imagined version of her as a parent which is impossible because... well...she wasn't one."

Tom tried to pull the words back from the air into his mouth, but he'd incanted them into being. Once they were out, they were his new truth.

"I can't believe Alle kept that from you," said Bryce, shaking his head.

"We built a relationship where Good Weather and Rain were the North Star in every decision. At least, I thought so. If I left, I don't know that she'd have survived it intact. It was self-preservation. Maybe she believed she was saving me heartache at the end. Maybe she was too selfish, too lost in Rain's spell. I can't live wondering. I want to bury that part and move on," replied Tom. His words seemed disconnected from him, but he meant every one of them.

"There may be hope for you yet, Tom Duncan," said Rio in the voice of a school marm.

Bryce pointed to the manila envelope.

"Did someone write a letter to Thames?" he asked.

Rio rose and inspected the inside of the envelope, shaking it to see if some stuck piece of parchment might come loose. But the manila envelope refused to offer any further gifts.

"Sounds like," said Rio, "we have an assignment before she wakes up."

CHAPTER 22

Tom would remember the next few hours of his life the way one remembers a silent movie. All of the dramatic action, but the flowing tributaries of voices completely mute. No technicolor, just varied shades of gray.

When they arrived back at the ICU, the doctor they'd spoken to earlier looked as though he was just about to abandon his search for the three friends. His expression, something Tom was sure the doctor practiced for occasions just such as this, already conveyed the news. Tom had seen it painted on the face of every well-wishing counselor at the recovery center. Once the doctor spoke, their devastation was instantaneous. The doctor offered something about a grief counselor and passed a card to Bryce. He was sorry for their loss.

The hospital staff were unforthcoming about arrangements. After some badgering, the three learned Thames had provided no instructions on final arrangements, so the hospital contacted her next of kin—an Aunt Ruth—who asked the staff to transfer the body to a funeral home for cremation. Rio bribed an orderly for the aunt's number.

After a few tries, they reached her, and Rio pleaded their case. She said it was inappropriate to cremate Thames' body considering her niece's beliefs. The others huddled around the phone as Rio spoke. Rio's arguments were well-reasoned and compassionate, presented with a Perry Mason finality, and Aunt Ruth shut them down immediately. She was a devout woman, she said, and whatever cult crap they'd been into, she wasn't going to enable it. Aunt Ruth hung up.

They rented rooms across from the hospital to give them time to sort things out. Tom called Anna to tell her that his friend died. Anna said she was sorry. She brought Terra to the phone, and the three of them talked for several minutes. Terra had seen an ad for a carnival. She shared every glorious detail with him. She wanted to see an elephant.

After a few minutes, Terra resumed her play date with Daniel Tiger, but Anna remained on the phone. What about his big chance to clear his name? she asked.

He missed it, he reported.

Maybe it was for the best because his friend needed him at the end, she said. He concurred. They exchanged I love yous. They hung up.

Tom searched for sorrow in himself, but he couldn't find it. People who experienced third degree burns often reported that they could not feel anything. Perhaps he was too depressed to know the depth of it. But he wasn't sure that was true. Maybe he'd finally let Alle go. Maybe that, not the letter, was Thames' final gift to him.

The group ordered Chinese and shared it in Tom's room. Rio wanted to know if he would give Anna the letter. He said, yes, because it was hers. He didn't intend to make the mistake Alle had. It was secrets that tore them apart at Good Weather. Rio was right. And he wasn't going to live that way.

They took up a game of Go Fish. They sat closer than necessary. They wanted to be together. Tom allowed himself to fade into the backdrop, not to be singular. It was a grand relief. A few hours later, Aunt Ruth phoned. She had gone through with the cremation, but she had decided to let the Good Weathers take the urn if they agreed to pay the funeral home. A deal was struck.

The next morning, they returned to the hospital. Bryce footed the bill. Others offered to help, but he wouldn't hear of it.

They spent the better part of breakfast debating which body of water would be the best place to say goodbye to their friend. The Cedar River eventually carried the day. They departed in the afternoon and took separate cars, but caravanned north to Black Hawk Park.

The sky overhead was vast and virtually cloudless as they pulled into the lot. Tom scanned around for swings, thinking of Terra, but he found none. Children clambered up and down on wooden equipment, chasing each other, squealing in delight. One parent kept a watchful eye on her daughter as she struggled with an oversized bow on the archery range. The temperature gauge in Tom's car read ninety-one, and heat radiated from the blacktop.

They parked the cars and piled out. The men stretched as Rio herded them together in the parking lot.

"I did some research last night, and what we're doing is perfectly legal as long as we scatter a few feet back from the water. To scatter remains in the water, we would need a permit and a bunch of other stuff that would take more time."

"I don't know the exact theology of Good Weather, but surely it's the gesture that counts in this case, right?" asked Bryce.

"We didn't cremate," said Tom, "so this is uncharted territory. But the community believed that once the *nephesh* was gone, the vessel was more or less a token to remember someone, a shell they'd shed on their way to the other coast."

Rio inspected the electron cloud of families picnicking, sun bathing, and playing Marco Polo in the water.

"It looks like there's a path in the woods. We'll follow that and pick a spot in sight of the water. She would have liked that."

As they made their way across the hot asphalt lot to the blacktop path then onto the trail, Tom considered the last time they'd trekked through the wild, not the portion when they faced dangerous weather, all of them high and fresh off a remembrance service. No, he replayed the several hours before they journeyed up Pine Bluff. He thought of Thames' eager, confident strides. She was meteoric. She'd had that intense velocity in every phase of life he'd known her, and he'd been honored to tail her momentum. He only wished now he had carried more of that weight that she so willingly placed on herself.

Tom was certain that when Rain approached the two young women who would become his first followers in the summer of 1992, his purpose had been to convert Alle to his cause. She checked all the boxes: youthful, energetic, pretty. But the true prize at that table in Raccoon Saloon was Thames. Alle was a skilled organizer and a persuasive speaker, but Thames exuded devotion to the cause from the minute Rain stepped into her life. She was a tornado which touched down briefly in a small bar in Iowa City, but there was no way it could contain her forever. She just needed someone to point in a direction.

When Good Weather migrated from Johnson St. to Shine or Rain, Rain announced in service that he intended to take on a personal attendant. No one believed there was ever a serious candidate besides Thames. Still, she greeted her coronation the following week with profound humility and gladness. She was luminous when Rain presented her on the stage.

And under her leadership, the camp seemed to flourish effortlessly. She organized the work teams, established the store as a means of revenue, and repaired the dilapidated buildings at camp. Rain took credit for these victories, but if a pipe exploded or a few ears of corn showed signs of blight, you called Thames, not Rain. Under her watchful eye, everything stayed on track as if it were compelled by some mysterious physics which operated at Shine or Rain alone.

In the end, when he'd found a way to control the community through drugs and fear, Rain sent Thames away because she was the one variable that could imbalance the chemical reaction he'd set in motion. She was the only one who could rival his authority at Good Weather. So, he plotted with Alle to take everything Thames loved from her and convinced her that it was her fault.

When Thames arrived on the next shore, he hoped the Good Weathers there would celebrate her. He hoped the whole Good Weather community would realize they shouldn't have trusted some huckster with a metal leg and a love of bloodshed, no matter how silver his tongue. He hoped that people were wiser on the sunnier coast.

Maybe there, Alle would be the person he'd imagined she was. If not, he could be content without ever seeing her again. This truth descended on him like some angelic intervention trickling through the cover of branches. He couldn't understand the scope of that epiphany now, but he was ready to begin wrestling with it soon.

Roughly a half a mile into the woods, they came into an open prairie where patches of black-eyed Susans upstretched their yellow heads to the sunshine. In the distance, the Cedar River gently drove its course past a sandbar and toward the campground. The voices of children still reached them.

"Alright, girl. You got it," said Rio.

They laid down their burdens and joined hands in a circle on the prairie. The circle felt so much smaller than when the weekend began. Tom led them in a recitation of the Doxology of Water:

> *"Oh true scripture, may I be ever obedient to you.*
> *Like the rain which washes the soil, saturate me till I overflow with truth.*
> *Clean me that I might be worthy of the estuary where I return.*
> *Like the flowing river, carry away the silt of my iniquity. Round me, till I am as you intend.*
> *May those who go before us over the lip of the world, praise you in Shamayim*
> *Do not forget us in your majesty, and do not let us forget one another."*

After the doxology was complete, Bryce took the urn out of the bag the hospital provided and passed it across the circle to Thames. She set this on the ground.

Rio withdrew a folded letter from her pocket, but did not begin to read it.

"Alright, girl, we noticed something when we opened your presents to us: it seems no one at Good Weather had the guts to put pen to paper for you before they all left for the other shore. But if you've learned anything about us this weekend, it's that we're willing to lay it all out there, for better or worse. So, we took up the task.

I'm gonna read you this letter then we'll spread these ashes. I hope you can hear this over the big party that's happening where you are," said Rio.

"You gotta tell her about our hook," whispered Bryce.

"Oh yeah! Each person wrote a paragraph, but we won't tell you who wrote which. We figured it might be fun for you to guess. We good now?" said Rio, turning to Bryce.

Bryce nodded and smiled. Rio began to read:

Dear Thames,

As this letter must invariably begin, we're going to miss you. I didn't know you as well as I would have liked. But I've never met anyone as honest as you. I think if everyone at Good Weather had resolved to live to your standard of truth, they might have been closer to Shamayim in this life than anyone has been. You coupled honesty with love. You loved people in the most profound way possible, even enough to coax this motley crew to gather and remember a community that might otherwise have been known for how they died, not how they lived. Tom wouldn't tell us what you asked him at the Silver Horse, but he said you restarted Single Query with a monster of a question. I'm jealous. So, I'm gonna take my shot in the new game, and I have a good one for you: what's it like on the brighter coast? I hope there's mountains to hike, a silver river crashing onto the rocks below, and I hope all the answers we need are there and all the people we love. I also desperately hope that the purses there are all oversized too.

"You gave yourself away," said Tom.

"Actually," replied Bryce, raising his hand, "that was me."

But he couldn't keep a straight face, and the whole crew burst into laughter. Rio playfully swatted at him.

"Don't forget, y'all: Bryce is still holding down Thames' job until we see her again," she said. "Now exercise some decorum!" Bryce frowned, which only evoked more laughter. When they settled down, Rio found her place again:

You almost certainly don't remember this, but once in the Shine or Rain days, we met when I came to the infirmary. I'd been planting all day in the fields—it was my first week on work shifts—and my hands were painfully cracked and dried. Whoever was in charge took one look at them and told me to toughen up, that we believed in Rough Hands here at Good Weather. I was just a kid, and I felt so embarrassed, especially because she announced this in front of the whole cabin.

I started to walk away, and you pulled me aside and handed me a pair of gloves. You told me never to be ashamed to ask for what I need. I'm not sure you even remember because it was the kind of thing I saw you do a hundred times at Good Weather. I'll miss you.

I guess I get the closing word here, but I'm uncertain I deserve it. I'm sorry, Thames, that we weren't with you at the bitter end. But thank you for making us a central part of your story. You said in your letter to us that you'd hoped to restore our faith. You did, but not in Rain or the true scripture. In the people of Good Weather and in you. Don't forget us. We love you without end. We'll see you on the sunnier coast.

Until then,
Your Friends

When she finished reading, Rio waited a moment. Tom felt the wind at their backs like a nipping puppy. Then Rio opened the urn and the remains of the vessel that Thames left behind fluttered in the air before settling on the prairie flowers and grasses. A gust flushed through the open field, and the ashes took to the air, upward toward a nimbus which hovered over a train trestle.

They all watched for a while, the heat pooling on their skin. Then Rio recollected the bag and placed it in her purse. She pointed in the direction of the cars and began walking. Bryce recessed across the field until, along with Rio, he vanished into the tree line again. Tom lingered just long enough to watch the ashes barrel out of sight on the breath of the northerly they were riding. Then he turned and followed after his friends, the August light falling heavier on him than he ever thought possible.

When they arrived back at the parking lot, most of the families had given up their activities and gone home. No more children running circles around the play equipment. No mother and daughter bonding over archery.

"I want to make a joke about what an uneventful weekend it's been," said Bryce, "but I worry it's in bad taste."

"Boy," said Rio, "what an uneventful weekend!"

"Well-played," he replied and wrapped an arm around her shoulder.

"Since I have big plans to ask the hard questions on the airwaves soon, I am going to throw one at you now. What happens to you, Bryce?" asked Rio.

"I go back to bachelor life in Waterloo," replied Bryce. "I only live a few hours from Tom. I figure we can check in every couple of years. Maybe we can move in together and star in some sort of *Real World* spin-off."

"I plan to be kicked out for sleeping with Steve G's girlfriend then lying about it," replied Tom.

"Look who's back with a little comedy! But it is my earnest hope that jokes about bad '90s television are not our final word to one another," laughed Rio.

"Well, I'll be joining you on the silver screen soon enough anyway, right?" said Bryce.

"While we're on that topic," said Tom. He reached into his pocket and handed his signed release back to Rio. He had decided somewhere between the Chinese and the game of Go Fish. He wanted to be with his friends again. The balance of issues was that simple to weigh.

"I am done with playing it cool now," Rio replied. She

danced around in impish delight, brandishing the signed release in her hand.

"Do you plan to see if Angela Downey is still interested?" asked Bryce.

"I doubt she is, and at this point, I don't think I am either. I figure the prospect of airing a tell-all interview with *the* Tom Duncan will give our budding young star here sufficient leverage to get this thing rolling."

"Not gonna lie," said Rio, "decorum be damned. I'm getting on the phone to my agent before we leave the parking lot. There will be squealing."

"Well, as long as you know that I intend to throw a fit if anyone has a larger dressing room and even half as much screen time as I, star of stage and screen, Tom Cornelius Duncan."

Tom pretended to throw back his hair.

Rio wrapped her arms around him.

"I hope you get to go home, Tom. And I hope your family reminds you how much you matter," said Rio.

Bryce piled on.

When they all brought themselves to let go, the sun had begun its descent. They each took to their cars, waving and honking. And after several minutes traveling back through the wilderness, they hit open highway, and, one-by-one, left each other behind.

CHAPTER 23

From the 2021 CBS Show *American Cult Stories,* Episode
1, "Our Story, My Story."

(The show opens with a fly-over of Pine Bluff. A slow,
acoustic version of "Only the Good Die Young" plays. The
vocalist is a woman with a thick Irish accent. It is winter,
and the towering trees are denuded of leaves. Huge
splotches of white are interrupted here and there by dark
metamorphic rocks. The camera passes over where the
camp once was. The camp structures have been replaced
with a series of glass, industrial buildings. The soccer field
is now a parking lot, and a handful of sedans cluster
around the spots closest to entry ways. Any evidence of the
chapel is gone. Then the show cuts to shots of a rural,
Brethren church, a synagogue, then a mosque. Rio speaks
as these images play.)

Rio: "Faith. It's the thread which has pulled the
tapestry of American civilization together for hundreds of
years. It has been the motive force behind some of our
greatest triumphs."

(The show cuts to footage of a Mennonite boy in

traditional garb serving in a soup kitchen, then a shot of Martin Luther King speaking in Birmingham, Alabama.)

"And the twisted ideology behind some of our worst tragedies."

(Images of the Manson family trial pass across the screen, then a clip of the first plane striking the Twin Towers plays. The show then cuts to Rio who sits in a director's chair. Her hair is short, but natural. She is clearly at home here.)

"Hello, I'm Elise Hernandez, but you can call me Rio. All my friends do. I'm a writer, a cancer survivor, and the host of *American Cult Stories*.

"For twenty-two years, I was also a member of the Good Weather community, a religious commune turned suicide cult. On this show, I'm going to bring you the stories of so many others who've seen faith at its best and, sadly, at its worst. But before I share their stories, I decided it was best to tell you my own and introduce you to the people who survived it.

"For anyone who has been living under a rock, let me get you up to speed: in the summer of 2019, the Good Weather community, unknowingly under the influence of intense psychotropic drugs fed to them by their leader Leonard Fairbanks, engaged in a mass suicide ritual where they slit one another's throats on a soccer field in Northeast Iowa. It was the largest mass suicide on U.S. soil—one hundred and thirty-seven people, including women and children.

"The event received unprecedented news coverage. Only a few days after the suicide, documentary director Don Burlington hired a film crew. Working on a hasty timeline, he directed and produced a documentary that was a smash hit on Netflix.

"It was so popular that Netflix executives requested that Burlington produce a special bonus episode some months after the show's release. He took on that project. As part of it, he interviewed a man named Russ Stevens, the brother-in-law of the sole survivor of the mass suicide—Tom Duncan. Stevens had a grudge against his brother-in-law, and he intimated, during the interview, that he had sources inside the Good Weather community who informed him that Tom Duncan hid a letter from his late wife that provided critical information about the health and well-being of their grandchild. He also suggested that Duncan was not a victim or survivor, but, in fact, helped mastermind the whole suicide plot."

(The documentary cuts to court sketches of Tom and a photo of a *New York Times* article entitled "Letter from Alle Duncan Uncovered.")

"In October of 2020, Duncan provided a letter to the *New York Times* from his late wife that not only evidenced that Stevens' claims were demonstrably false, but also that Lisa Duncan had, in fact, hidden the letter in question from Tom. Netflix immediately removed the episode from its streaming service and, as of the time of the taping of this show, is considering shelving the documentary as a whole, according to a representative for the company.

"Duncan filed slander claims against Burlington and Stevens. Both settled out of court.

"As the sole survivor of the suicide, Tom Duncan has faced intense scrutiny over how he managed to live and whether he played a role in hatching and implementing the suicide plot. But in order to truly understand what happened at Good Weather, first we need to hear what life was like for those closest to its members."

(The show switches to a shot of Bryce and Rio who sit at a white table on a patio together. Ivy climbs the trellis behind them. A caption identifies Bryce.)

Rio: "Bryce, can you share a little bit about how your father's relationship with the Good Weather community and Leonard Fairbanks affected you?"

Bryce: (Takes a deep breath) "Negatively. It ruined the possibility of a meaningful relationship with my father in his lifetime. That is an accurate blanket answer, but I suspect that you will ask me to drill down on that."

Rio: "You know me too well."

Bryce: "The question is tricky because it's difficult to say what sort of man my father might have been if he had never met Leonard Fairbanks. Everyone who dealt with my father as a businessman described him as a tough customer. As a black entrepreneur in Iowa, he faced overt and covert racism and systemic inequality that, while still present today, was virtually insurmountable at the time. I think the cost of defeating the colossuses in his own life made him colder with me than he ever meant to be. I think it hollowed him out, which is why Rain and Good Weather spoke to him. He needed something to fill that void.

"My dad didn't require any help to be a distant father, but Good Weather gave him an ideology to support his coldness."

Rio: "It sounds like your father valued a different feature of Good Weather than many of the believers there did."

Bryce: "In a way, I think that's true. At Good Weather, he was admired. In his mind, he had saved the community when they'd been all but driven out by the citizens of Iowa

City. He was an essential servant of the prophet. And in Fairbanks' belief system, the racists who'd looked down their noses at him, who had denied him loans and kept him out of the country club, were headed straight for damnation because they couldn't see the truth when it was looking them right in the eyes. It was an ideal fit for my dad's worldview.

"As a parent, I think he visualized what was ahead for me, and it terrified him. But rather than nurturing me, he worked to toughen me up for the fight. That's a great strategy if you want to train a professional boxer, but I was a little kid who was terribly afraid. And when I looked to my father for reassurance, he ordered me to recite my scriptures and showed me how to fire a gun. One thing I have learned in my years of therapy is that emotional worries aren't always solved with practical solutions. That's something that was very hard for my father to understand."

Rio: "What did his relationship with Good Weather cost your father? Do you know for sure?"

Bryce: "It might be easier to ask what it didn't cost him. Fairbanks drained my dad's bank accounts. He convinced him to give up his family. If my father had any aspiration besides bankrolling a megalomaniac, it was never to be."

Rio: "I think it might be tough for our audience to understand how you can be justifiably angry at Rain and what he did to your family, how he turned your father against you and himself, and still remain intimately connected to the surviving members of the Good Weather community. Can you help them understand?"

Bryce: "I can try." (He turns to look directly at the

camera.) "I should start by saying that it has taken me a long time to reach a moment where I can separate those feelings out. And some days, I'm just not capable of that kind of nuance. On those days, I am so angry and sad. It's nearly impossible to see anything but shadows. All of us have moments like that, of course.

"It might be easier if you first understand a truth I've known since I was a child: Good Weather was a family. Members took care of each other, set boundaries, got in fights, worked it out, and loved each other through some very difficult times.

"Now imagine a nightmare scenario. Imagine that your father committed a violent murder. Imagine he killed another family member and then took his own life. Imagine that he perpetrated these acts in such a horrible way that they appeared on every major news network for weeks on end.

"If that absolutely horrible event happened to you, after all the grief, sadness, and doubt, you'd likely still find yourself thinking back on all those happy memories of family picnics, vacations, weddings. But you would find it tough to separate them from the darkness of that violence. If you're like me, this feeling would haunt you for a long time. But after a while, you would realize that by cutting yourself off, you let your father take even more from you. You might decide to reconnect with those people you loved. You might decide to fight the darkness back into the corners of your psyche so there can be somewhere for you as a person to live again."

Rio: "Well-said. I have one more question for you, and I've saved the best for last. Rumor has it that you are bethrothed to one Sandy Dawson, another former member of the Good Weather community. When someone asks, how do describe how you met?"

(A wind picks up and gusts Rio's notes, and Bryce races and catches them.)

Bryce: "Well, for those nosey enough to ask," (Bryce jokingly glares at Rio.) "I am honest. We met because we both lost people we loved. If you think that is any weirder than meeting someone by filling out an online profile or swiping right or left on your cell phone, I encourage you to take a long, hard look at your life." (He laughs.)

(The screen briefly fades to black then the show cuts to footage of Tom's police interviews, then some of the reel from the orientation video, then a shot of Tom making his way through a sea of paparazzi after his slander case. Rio voices-over the montage.)

Rio: "Tom Duncan is the lone survivor of the mass suicide at Camp Shine or Rain. He took part in the suicide ceremony, but his wife's attempt to cut his throat was not fatal. After he was rescued by the Sheriff's department and EMT's, he recovered while facing the horrific reality that everyone he knew he was dead, that his way of life was over.

"However, the nightmare did not end there. After Don Burlington's documentary broadcast the claims of ex-Detective Harold Dodson, who believed—despite evidence to the contrary—that Tom was complicit in drugging the Good Weather community, Duncan's private life was invaded by journalists seeking to tie him to the plot of which he was a victim. Though he was never charged with a crime, Duncan became a widely disliked figure. This public scorn was made worse when Russ Stevens—his brother-in-law—stated in an interview with Don

Burlington that Duncan withheld a letter from his wife about their daughter's troubled pregnancy in order to keep her from leaving the community.

"After several months of public derision, Duncan evidenced the falsehood of Stevens' claim in the press and in court. His vindication eased public and media scrutiny of him. He still faces personal challenges related to his role in the events of August 7th, 2019. But he now lives in Des Moines near his daughter. He works at a local restaurant and is a caregiver for his granddaughter. This is the first public interview Duncan has ever agreed to provide."

(The camera focuses in on a dark studio. Tom sits under a spotlight holding a series of notes in his lap. Rio is in her director's chair across from him. Tom has begun balding a bit, but the bags under his eyes are no longer evident. His wears a white dress shirt without tie, a pair of jeans, and sneakers.)

Rio: "First, I'd like to thank you for agreeing to this interview with us. I know your relationship with the media hasn't always been cordial."

Tom: "At one point, I held the dubious distinction of appearing in a top ten list of 'most disliked Americans.' So, I'm not sure why you even invited me on your program."

Rio: (Stifles a laugh) "I would be letting my audience down if I didn't ask the question that has made many members of the public so angry at you: were you complicit with Rain in drugging the Good Weather community?"

Tom: (Pauses for a moment, clearly considering his response) "Everything I told the police was truthful, and I stand by the information I provided in my interview. I was not complicit in any way. I was a victim. I am going to offer that first so that there's no ambiguity.

"But it's clear that the answers I provided in that interview aren't enough for everyone. So, I have two things to offer to the American public. First, I want you to understand that Rain was a master manipulator. He could make you feel loved and valued with just a word or leave you in a broken waste with the same. Sending emails from my computer was likely one of hundreds of schemes he concocted to flag blame away from himself.

"Secondly, to the families of everyone who lost loved ones at Shine or Rain, I want to tell you how sorry I am that I was not well enough to stop what happened. The people who we lost were my friends, and their absence lives in me every minute of every day."

Rio: "I think that's important for everyone to hear. Thank you. I wonder: how has life changed for you since Netflix withdrew their support of Don Burlington's bonus episode and, to some extent, the documentary as a whole?"

Tom: "My odds of being accosted by a stranger at the park are lower. It seems easier for the people I meet to understand me as a survivor, which is important because I have struggled to understand that myself. I still feel incredible guilt for what I did and didn't do. That is the poison that has never left my system even after all the drugs wore off. Not a day goes by that I don't remember the faces of one of those one hundred and thirty-seven friends and wonder what I could have done differently. But I can't live that way, Janus-faced, and if I owe our friends who passed over anything, it's that: to be an active part of this life they were robbed of."

Rio: (She pauses for a moment.) "Do you have regrets?"

Tom: "More than I can even count."

Rio: "What do you do with them?"

Tom: "An honest but unsatisfying answer is that I try not to let them rule me. Because if I let them be my anchor, they're going to pull down me and everyone I love. It's not easy. It's not. The best any of us can do is live like it matters and pray for forgiveness."

Rio: "What else do you think our audience should know about Good Weather and the people who died there?"

(Tom removes the notes from his lap and collects a series of printed papers beside him. This is a question he seems glad to answer. He pushes his glasses up his nose.)

Tom: "I came prepared!" (He merrily waves his sheets in the air.) "On August 6th, 2019, many members of the Good Weather community wrote letters that they believed would be mailed to family or friends. Those letters went undelivered for a long time, but last year a now-deceased and beloved community member named Katie Hunt willed the letters to a group of fellow survivors. I was proud to be among them. Over the course of several months, we delivered each letter to its recipient. Sometimes the missives were welcome. Other times they were not.

"We wrote those family and friends and asked if they would allow us to share these letters on this show. We hope the Good Weather community can be remembered as a group of complicated, complex individuals who lived with and loved one another before they were victims in some ways of themselves and in other ways of Leonard Fairbanks, a man they trusted and admired. We are grateful to those who've allowed us to share these messages."

(Tom glances over at Rio. She offers a small smile and nods. Tom opens the first letter and allows a breath of fresh air to fill him. Then he begins to read.)

ABOUT
ATMOSPHERE PRESS

Atmosphere Press is an independent, full-service publisher for excellent books in all genres and for all audiences. Learn more about what we do at atmospherepress.com.

We encourage you to check out some of Atmosphere's latest releases, which are available at Amazon.com and via order from your local bookstore:

The Embers of Tradition, a novel by Chukwudum Okeke

Saints and Martyrs: A Novel, by Aaron Roe

When I Am Ashes, a novel by Amber Rose

Melancholy Vision: A Revolution Series Novel, by L.C. Hamilton

The Recoleta Stories, by Bryon Esmond Butler

Voodoo Hideaway, a novel by Vance Cariaga

Hart Street and Main, a novel by Tabitha Sprunger

The Weed Lady, a novel by Shea R. Embry

A Book of Life, a novel by David Ellis

It Was Called a Home, a novel by Brian Nisun

Grace, a novel by Nancy Allen

Shifted, a novel by KristaLyn A. Vetovich

ABOUT THE AUTHOR

Kyle McCord is the author of six books, including National Poetry Series Finalist, *Magpies in the Valley of Oleanders* (Trio House Press, 2016) and *X-Rays and Other Landscapes* (Trio House Press, 2019). He has work featured in *AGNI, Blackbird, Boston Review, The Gettysburg Review, The Harvard Review, The Kenyon Review, Ploughshares, TriQuarterly,* and elsewhere. He has received grants and awards from The Academy of American Poets, The Vermont Studio Center, and the Baltic Writing Residency.

He serves as Executive Editor of Gold Wake Press and teaches at Drake University in Des Moines. He is married to visual artist Lydia McCord. They have an adorable son named August.

Made in the USA
Monee, IL
01 August 2021